T0103925

strange eyes

Part 1 of 'Taz' Trilogy

PAM TUNBRIDGE

Trafford rev. 02/18/2014

Trafford
PUBLISHING®   www.trafford.com

North America & international
toll-free: 1 888 232 4444 (USA & Canada)
fax: 812 355 4082

Strange Eyes

Part 1 of 'Taz' Trilogy

Pam Tunbridge

Illustrated by
Nancy Darke

Cover Design & Typesetting
Jan Whitworth

By the same author

The Alphabet Gang
Part 2 of 'Taz' Trilogy

Taz
Part 3 of 'Taz' Trilogy

Contents

PROLOGUE

It was six o' clock in the morning and as usual it was the click of the hot water heater that woke him; and as usual he jumped out of bed, full of the joys of spring and ran to the door. Peering out he could see a cloudless sky and the sun just coming up over the trees across the field from his house, weather wise it was going to be a lovely day and he briefly wondered what the day would bring for him. Still, no time to waste, the fine day was calling and off he went.

He raced across the field as fast as he could, the cool morning air, brushing all the sleepy cobwebs from his mind. He frightened a pheasant, which burst out of the long grass in front of him, squawking and flapping its way across the field and into a garden across the track. Although it made him jump too, he had a little grin to himself, he liked to chase and frighten them too.

He was heading to his favourite watching and resting place; a huge oak tree, not far from the track which separated the field from a few large houses. Once there he would hurl himself down on his tummy to watch the world go by. If he looked to his left, the track disappeared through a large farm gate and into a thick wood, beyond that was a small holiday park, run by a local farm. If he looked to his right, to the start of the track, he could see the main road and the pond at the edge of the field, where moor hens and coots were beginning to nest again. Straight ahead of him, on the other side of the track, was Ben's house. He called it Ben's house, because 'Ben' was the only name he ever heard when people were talking or calling to him.

Sometimes he called to Ben, who never answered or came to play, they just stared at each other.

Ben's house was hidden down a long drive behind more big trees, he'd like to have gone and had a closer look, but he didn't want to upset anyone and get told off. Each side of it were more big houses, the people who lived in them spoke to him if they were out walking and saw him, but usually they came and went in their cars, and didn't see him.

There wasn't a lot of world here to watch go by, but it was very peaceful. He could see different birds flying back and forth, building nests at this time of year; sometimes he saw a rabbit or hare, they always ran away when they realised he was there and squirrels shot up the nearest trees when they saw him, but never up his tree. He listened to birds singing, the occasional domestic noise from the houses, the wind ruffling leaves in the trees, and today the rattling of milk bottles and the droning of the milk cart as the milkman drove up the track to the house, just out of sight round the corner. Whenever the milkman saw him, he always called out and waved his hand, which was always holding a small edible treat, usually a biscuit with cream in the middle. He didn't want to get up today, it was so warm and cosy under his oak tree as the sunlight had just stretched a finger of warmth towards him. Anyway it might be one of the days the milkman called at his house, so he could catch up with him there.

He knew by the time of the year, that it wouldn't be long before the track became busier. Easter was coming and there'd be lots of people arriving in cars, some towing caravans, to spend early holidays at the campsite. He might recognise some of the people, who came back year after year. He wondered if they would remember him. It was always nice to meet new friends as well as old ones, which reminded him he may see the postman in a while, who always gave him something to eat and said 'hope that won't spoil your breakfast.'

Of course it didn't he could always manage breakfast, after all he was a growing boy. Today though, the postman must be a bit late, because he could hear the distant school clock, chiming half past six. Breakfast time, he jumped up, and fast as he could he ran back home, where he hoped it would be waiting for him.

PART 1

JACK

Chapter 1

He was cold, he was wet and he was totally fed up. 'Stupid holiday,' he said out loud, 'stupid rain, stupid, stupid Mum making me come here.' Jack scuffed through the leaves on the floor of the woods. His hands were shoved deep into the pockets of his jeans, his shoulders hunched over and his head was hanging low, to try and keep the rain off his face. As if all that wasn't bad enough, he was lost.

Muttering to himself about how everything was stupid and boring without Dad here, Jack wandered further and further into the trees, trying to find a bit of shelter. Eventually he just sank down onto the wet ground, at the foot of a large tree, buried his face into his knees and started crying.

He didn't know how long he'd been sitting there, when he felt a warm, wet, wriggling thing on the back of his hand. He jerked his head up, swiping his tears away with one hand as he snatched the other back and found himself looking into two very strange eyes; one was brown the other blue. Jack jumped to his feet, and looked down to see a scruffy grey and white collie dog staring up at him with those amazing eyes and twitching its black shiny wet nose. 'Hello you,' Jack said nervously, pushing back up against the tree and hoping the dog was friendly. The dog cocked its head to one side and looked at him, then reached forward and pushed its nose into Jack's hand.

Realising the dog probably wasn't going to tear his face off, he let the collie lick his fingers; then he gently scratched behind the dog's ears, murmuring softly to **IT**, he loved dogs but had never been allowed to have one. Suddenly it ran off a few yards and turned back to look at him. Jack just stood watching, then the dog ran up to him again and nudged his hand. I think he wants me to follow, thought the boy, if I do, he might lead me out of these woods. Feeling slightly happier, Jack squared his shoulders and followed the collie.

The rain was still pouring down and he could barely hold his head up enough to follow the dog, but he managed to keep its back legs in sight as it ran in front of him. He was just wondering if he was being led further into wet murky woods, when the dog vanished around a bend in the path. Jack ran a bit faster and panting in pursuit, he saw the dog jump over a small fence surrounding a rather overgrown garden, it then ran up to a dilapidated looking barn. Jack couldn't see a gate, so he also jumped the fence and ran to the open door, which the dog had pushed open with its nose. It was now standing in the doorway, wagging its tail and looking at Jack.

What should I do, go in and risk being caught and yelled at by the owner, thought Jack? But then he decided that no one sensible would be wandering around their garden in this. Taking a deep breath he ran inside and looked around. It was quite a small barn, with old straw bales stacked in one corner, some ancient looking, rusty tools hanging from hooks in the rafters and a tatty, wicker dog basket with a rather worn blanket in it. The roof was high and had a few holes in it, but the barn was mostly dry though musty smelling.

'Here dog,' said Jack patting his leg and it wandered over. 'What's your name then?' He knelt down and under the thick fur of the dog's neck he found a choke chain with a worn tag on it. Squinting in the gloom, Jack rubbed his thumb over the tag and made out the letters T and A. There was another letter which could've been a wonky L, but Jack thought TAL wasn't a likely name for the dog, so he went through the alphabet and came up with, TAB, TAD, TAF, TAG, TAM, TAN, TAP, TAR, TAX and TAZ. 'Hmm,' said Jack, 'I think TAM is good, let's try that.'

He stood up and wandered around a bit, then squatting down he faced the dog and said, 'Hey Tam, here boy or are you a girl.' The dog just looked at him, as if to say, 'A girl?' After a few more useless tries Jack said, 'How about TAZ,' really loudly, immediately the dog ran over and rubbed its wet head against Jack's knee. 'Hey,' laughed Jack, 'Pleased to meet you Taz, with a name like that you must be a boy, I'm Jack.' And so saying he sat down on a straw bale, and patted the space beside him, hoping the dog would jump up. But Taz turned away, went over to his bed and pulled the scruffy blanket out and dragged it back to Jack, then he jumped up, circled round a couple of times and curled into a ball next to Jack's leg. Putting one arm over Taz's back and the musty blanket over his legs, Jack leaned back, listening to the rain rattling on the roof. He gradually warmed up and while still stroking the furry body next to him he fell asleep.

It was the sudden silence that woke him, the rain had stopped and peering through the door, Jack could see patches of blue sky. He glanced at his watch, four o' clock, Mum would be angry and worried, and he'd been gone about three hours. With all this running through his head, he briefly forgot about Taz. He turned back to the hay bale he'd been asleep on, but there was no sign of the dog. 'Taz, come on boy, where are you?' called Jack as he ran out of the door, but there was no response.

Oh well maybe we'll meet up again if I can find out where I am, he thought to himself.

Now that the rain had stopped and Jack could run with his head up and see where he was going, he found that he was in the large garden of a small cottage. Making his way towards the back door, Jack hoped he wouldn't meet anyone and get shouted at, for trespassing. He'd say he was lost and needed directions, but the place seemed to be deserted. He glanced through a small window in the door, above what looked like a large cat flap, and saw a kitchen. There was a dog basket on the floor, Taz must have an indoor and an outdoor bed, thought Jack, I wonder where he is. Rounding the side of the cottage, he suddenly realised where he was. The front door of the cottage faced onto the field, the other side of that was the track that led back to the Holiday Park at the farm. Thank goodness, thought Jack, I'm not very far away from the caravan and the telling off, I'll get from Mum. He ran wondering if he'd be sent to bed with no supper, have his TV time stopped or even worse, *grounded*. If that happened, he wouldn't get to see Taz again.

Chapter 2

Putting on his best 'I'm sorry,' face, Jack went into the caravan, but before he could say anything, Mum looked up from where she was writing something and said, 'Hi Jack, had a nice time, did you get soaked?'

'Um, yeah, thanks, I did get a bit wet, but I found shelter under trees,' he answered. Why was Mum being so nice? 'Aren't you cross with me for being late?'

'Not cross,' said his mum, 'a bit worried, but as we've been here before, I thought you'd met up with some old friends.

'No just exploring to see if anything has changed since we were last here, it mostly looks the same.'

'It's been two and a half years since then and you were only nine.' said Mum. Jack just nodded and turned away, so she wouldn't see his eyes fill with tears. The last time they were all here, Dad was with them, but he'd been killed, in a car accident. Jack hadn't wanted to come back here, he thought he'd have too many sad memories, but if his mum could face up to it, so could he. Keeping his back to her, he said, 'What's for dinner, shall I put the table together?'

'If you think you can manage,' said mum smiling, 'remember when Dad didn't put the leg in properly and it collapsed while we were playing cards?' They both laughed.

'Yeah, Dad got really cross, 'cos he was winning and we made him reshuffle and deal again. They were good times weren't they Mum?'

'They will be again Jack, we just have to make the most of what we have,' she replied quietly and Jack noticed that her eyes were getting a bit wet too.

'What shall we do tomorrow? Have you planned anything?' he said, to change the subject, he didn't like to see her being sad. He hoped she hadn't as he wanted to go and find Taz. Before Dad had died they'd talked about *maybe* getting a dog, but since then, Mum had to work full time. It wouldn't be fair to leave a dog on its own for so long during the day.

'Well I've got to sort out some stuff at reception first, and then go to the supermarket, so I'd like some help carrying the shopping please.' Jack groaned and said if they went really early, they'd have the rest of the day to do interesting stuff.

'I might get to see some old friends,' he said, thinking about Taz.

'We'll see,' said Mum, 'come on sort that table out ready for dinner.'

Later as he lay in his high bunk, behind the curtain, Jack listened to the sounds of his Mum tidying up, then the rustle of papers as she'd brought some work with her. She was a teacher and was probably marking books, which she seemed to do a lot of during school holidays. He was glad she was a teacher; it meant they could be together in the holidays. Although he would be going to High School in September, he didn't think it was un-cool to be with his Mum, anyway she needed him now, he was the man of the family. He hadn't told her about Taz, because he didn't want her to think he was still upset about not having a dog of his own. Anyway it wouldn't hurt to have a secret.

As he snuggled down in his sleeping bag, Jack remembered how good and safe he'd felt when he'd put his arm around the dog, before nodding off in the barn—and then Jack's eyes shot open, he was wide awake, a thought had crossed his mind. When he'd woken up alone, on the hay bale, he'd no longer had the dog's blanket over his legs; it was back in the basket. Well, what a dog, thought Jack, he must have tidied up. I'll definitely persuade Mum to let me have one, I can train it to help tidy my room. With this funny idea in his head, he fell asleep.

Chapter 3

By 9 o' clock the following morning, Jack was hopping from one foot to the other in the holiday camp office, impatient to get going. His mother was trying to sort out some day trip or other, for later in the week. 'Stop being a fidget, Jack,' she said, 'go look at the notice board see if there are any of the usual, sport or challenge competitions coming up.' Jack wandered off, nothing he saw on the board interested him much. In the past he and his dad had made their own fun or teamed up with other kids and their dads to do stuff.

There was a painting competition, to be judged at the end of the summer season. No good for me, we won't be here then, he said to himself. There was a fancy dress competition at the kid's party on Easter Monday, but Jack considered himself too old for that, he also saw a poster advertising a talk and film about the local woodland and shore, wildlife. He considered himself too young to enjoy that. At last Mum called him over and then they were off to visit the big superstore, where they'd shopped before, when they came here, on holiday.

As usual, lots of memories involving Dad came back and Jack found himself saying a lot of 'do you remembers?' Mum just smiled and now and again added some of her own. Finally they finished the shopping, got through the checkout and Jack jumped on the wheel bar of the trolley and scooted over towards their car, he looked back towards his mother, expecting her to tell him not to. Unfortunately he didn't turn back in time to see where he was going and with a sudden jolt he ran the trolley into the back of a parked car, a very dusty Land Rover. All the air was knocked from Jack's chest and as he bent over the trolley gasping, Mum ran up and began to apologise to the tall man who was just getting out of the car. What about me, I can't breathe, Jack was thinking.

Strong hands pulled him upright, from the trolley and a deep voice said, 'Breath deeply son, relax and take deep breaths.' Jack looked up into the man's concerned looking face. He tried to say 'I'm sorry,' but just a gasp came out.

'It's ok take it easy,' said the man, then turning to mum he added, 'I think he'll live.'

'I've told him hundreds of times not to do that,' she said 'has he damaged your car?'

'I think this old thing has put up with a lot more, than what your boy has done, these Land Rovers are tough old cars,' said the man. His eyes were now twinkling and Jack thought he was trying not to laugh at the gasping, wheezing noises coming from Jack's mouth. Mum was still looking distressed and embarrassed and wrote her name and phone number on a piece of paper and handed it to the man.

'Please let me pay for any damage,' she said, 'we're staying at the Alton Holiday Park, until next Saturday.'

Jack's breathing was settling down and he said, 'I'm very sorry, my pocket money can help pay towards it.'

The man rubbed the mud off the bumper where the trolley had hit it and said, 'I can't see anything wrong, but I'll let you know if there is, meanwhile let's forget it.' Still smiling at Mum, he put the piece of paper she'd written on, in his pocket and walked off towards the store.

For the next hour, she was very quiet and only spoke to Jack in a cross voice, telling him to load then unload the shopping back at the caravan. When he tried to apologise again, she just held up her hand for him to be quiet. Jack went and lay on his bunk, he was worried about how much he might have to pay for damaging the car, and he only had £60 saved up for holidays, the car might cost hundreds to repair.

Eventually Mum asked him if he wanted a ham or cheese sandwich for lunch. Jack didn't dare say 'both,' if she was talking to him again he didn't want to upset things. 'Cheese please and I'm really sorry,' he gabbled quickly. Mum turned to look at him, the corners of her mouth twitching as though she was trying not to laugh.

'Come here Jack,' she said, 'hold out your hand.' He slid off his bunk and shuffled across, one hand held out, awaiting his punishment. Then, to his surprise, 'Give me five Jack, apology accepted and *don't* do it again, if that car is damaged and costs more than what you have saved, I'll stop your pocket money, until the debt's paid off.'

'Ok,' groaned Jack, 'but I might be an old man by then.'

'What makes you think I'll be giving an old man pocket money?' she said and they both smiled at each other.

'Can I go exploring after lunch please?' asked Jack,

'Only if you eat your lunch, clear your plate away and give me a hug,' said Mum. 'If I can have a couple of hour's peace and quiet, I can finish my homework and relax for the rest of our holiday. Just behave, take care and don't do anything silly or dangerous and . . .'

'Don't talk to strangers,' Jack finished. He wondered if she'd think Taz was a stranger. He certainly had strange eyes.

Chapter 4

Jack made his way through the holiday park, out onto the lane and across the field to Taz's house. The weather was better today, but a bit chilly, so he was wearing his waterproof jacket, just in case. He was a few steps away from the fence around the garden, when he saw Taz just running off, away towards the trees. Jack ran after him, calling, 'Taz, Taz, wait for me,' but the dog kept going. When Jack reached the trees he saw the grey and white fluffy tail disappearing through the undergrowth, he rushed after it and finally found Taz lying on his tummy with his nose buried in a bunch of brambles; his tail was wagging across the path, brushing leaves and twigs about.

'Hey boy, coming to play?' said Jack ruffling Taz behind his ears and picking up a stick. He threw it deeper into the undergrowth and said, 'Come on Taz, fetch.' The dog briefly looked at Jack and went back to snuffling in the brambles and after another waste of time throw, the boy got down next to him and said, 'What is it, what have you found?' Taz backed off a bit and Jack moved some of the brambles, pricking his fingers on their sharp thorns. 'Eeyowch!' he yelled, jumping up, shaking his hand and putting his fingers in his mouth. 'Look what you made me do.' Taz sat up on his hind legs cocked his head on one side and looked at the boy with his strange eyes then he lay down and scrabbled in the brambles again.

'What *is* it?' Jack repeated and covering his hand with the sleeve of his jacket he pushed the brambles aside. At first all he could see were bits of twig, dead bracken and

13

wet leaves, then the leaves moved and he heard a tiny, pitiful squeaky noise. Jack didn't want to get bitten by anything, so he found a small stick and gently pushed the undergrowth aside. Taz immediately stuck his nose in the cleared space before Jack could see what was there. 'Come out of the way Taz,' he said but the dog grabbed something in his mouth and started to pull it out. Whatever it was started squeaking again and Jack could see a bedraggled looking little body, wriggling in the dog's soft mouth, it looked like a kitten.

'Ok well done boy, let me help now,' said Jack, he could see that the creature's leg was caught in something. Taz let Jack take the poor little thing from his mouth, it *was* a kitten and it felt very cold and bony to Jack. Not worrying about prickles now, Jack felt under the kitten and realised one of its back legs was caught on a piece of twine, like fishermen used. He took off his jacket, laid it on the ground and put the kitten on it, then pulling at the twine he gradually released it from the soft earth.

'Good boy, Taz, let's take this kitten home and get some help for it,' said Jack, carefully wrapping the little body in his jacket. It was very quiet now and Jack hoped it could be saved.

They ran to Taz's house, but as no one answered the door, Jack thought the people must be at work, so he knew he had to take it back to the caravan and his mother. He hoped she'd finished her work now, after what had happened this morning, he didn't want to upset her again. He ran fast and shouted out to Taz, but the dog had stayed at his own house.

Concentrating on the kitten Jack burst through the door and shouted, 'Mum, Mum,' and made her jump.

'Whatever is it Jack?' she said crossly as the boy unwrapped his jacket. 'Oh my word, what's happened,' she looked at the poor little kitten.

'I found it in the woods, its leg was caught up and it's really cold and hungry and I don't want it to die,' said Jack in one breath. Mum took the kitten from him and gently stroked its face, it squeaked and looked up at her.

'Jack, run to the office and find out if there's a local vet,' she said,' I'll try and give it some warm milk.' Jack rushed off while Mum poured some milk into a dish with a bit of warm water, from the kettle. She dipped a finger in the liquid and held it to the kitten's nose, which twitched, and then a little pink tongue came out and licked her finger. She did this several times and then as the kitten seemed to get stronger, she tried to spoon some milk into the tiny mouth.

Jack was back in a few minutes, with the name of the vet and directions of where it was. 'Is it ok Mum, can we go now?' he said breathlessly, grabbing the car keys, 'the lady in the office is going to ring the vet to let them know we're on our way.' The kitten appeared to have fallen asleep, so Mum wrapped it in a towel and handed it to Jack.

'Be careful of its leg, I'm not sure if it's broken,' she said, 'just hold it gently on your lap in the car and we'll hope that it can be saved.

Looking at the directions to the vet surgery, she realised she knew where it was, they always drove past it on their way to the superstore, it wasn't very far away. Happier now that she knew where they were going, they set off.

Chapter 5

After a few, 'Are we there yet?' and 'Can't we go faster?' from Jack they finally pulled into the car park at the vets. As he made to leap out of the car, his mother said, 'Sit still, let me open the door for you, or you might harm the kitten.'

'Hurry up then Mum,' the impatient boy replied.

Once out of the car he walked quickly to the door and waited for his mum to open it for him. He had a quick glance around and saw two people with a cat basket sitting in the waiting area and a lady behind the reception desk who was wearing a green overall, like nurses wore.

Before he could say anything, she stood up and said, 'You must be Mrs. Knight and Jack, Sheila from the Holiday Park phoned ahead, she said you have an emergency.'

'Yes, thanks so much for letting us come straight over,' said mum, 'I don't think this poor little mite will last much longer.'

'Don't *say* that Mum, it'll be fine now we're here,' said Jack with a slight catch in his voice.

'Our vet, Mr. Mark Carter said you can go straight through,' said the nurse and she pressed a button on her phone to let the vet know they were there.

The kitten felt very still in Jack's arms and he rushed to the door with the sign 'Mark Carter' on it. Once again his Mum opened the door for him and they stepped inside. The vet, a tall man was washing his hands at the sink and just as Jack started to say, 'I've got this really sick . . .' the man turned round to face him and Jack's heart started thumping, he turned to mum, who faintly said 'Oh.'

The man standing before them was the one whose car Jack had crashed into that morning. He smiled and said, 'We meet again, I'm Mark Carter, what have you brought me?' Quickly recovering from his surprise, Jack explained that he'd found the kitten in some undergrowth and that its leg was caught on some twine.

'It's very small and skinny, please help it, Mum gave it a bit of milk,' he said handing the small towel wrapped bundle to the vet.

His mother didn't say anything, Jack wondered if she was worrying about paying for the car and then he thought, will we have to pay for this kitten?

Before he could voice any of these worries, the vet, who had been carefully checking the little body, gently removed the twine from its leg, and said' 'It's a boy, I don't think this little chap has any broken bones, but his leg will be very sore. He's obviously been struggling to free himself and the twine has cut into the skin. I'll give him an antibiotic injection and he also needs a good meal, he looks to me as though he's old enough to have been weaned.'

'What's weaned?' asked Jack

Both the vet and his Mum answered at the same time.

'He can eat solid food now.' Mum said.

'He doesn't need his mother's milk anymore,' said the vet.

'What will happen to him now?' asked Jack worriedly.

'He does seem young to be on his own,' said Mark, 'maybe you can ask the holiday park people to put a 'found' notice up in the office, Jack.'

'S'pose no one claims him?'

'We'll worry about that later,' meanwhile he can stay here over night, so I can keep an eye on him and if he's stronger tomorrow, I'll take him to a lady I know who looks after cats and finds new homes for them.'

Before he could stop himself Jack said, 'Can I come with you please?'

'Jack, don't be cheeky, I'm so sorry, Mr. Carter,' Mum said going red in the face. The vet laughed, 'Call me Mark and yes Jack you can come along, your Mum too if she likes.'

'I just want to make sure he's going to be ok, can I give him a name?' said the worried boy.

Mum stopped looking so flustered now and said, 'I'd love to come along tomorrow if it isn't too much trouble and my name's Lisa.'

Solemnly the vet stuck out his hand to Mum then to Jack, 'Pleased to meet you both,' he said. 'If you come here about midday tomorrow, I'll know by then what the situation with the kitten is,'

'He's called Tam,' interrupted Jack, 'and thanks Mr. Carter, what do you think I should pay for first, your car or the kitten?'

'You can call me Mark, too,' the vet smiled, 'and I'll let you know tomorrow about payments, now let me get this patient fed.'

Chapter 6

Jack was quiet in the car on the way back to the caravan a lot of things had happened in the short time they'd been here. He'd got lost, he'd met Taz, he'd crashed a trolley, he'd helped rescue a kitten, now called Tam, made another new friend—at least he hoped so—Mark Carter and he was going to meet a 'cat' lady tomorrow. He thought his Mum seemed calmer too, she was usually arranging things to keep him happy and now someone else had stepped in and arranged something for them both, tomorrow. Thinking back, Jack had noticed that Mum's eyes had sparkled a bit when she'd told Mark her name and how his handshake lasted a bit longer on her hand than on his.

Hmm, I shall have to keep an eye on her. He glanced at his mother she was staring ahead at the road. 'He seems nice, doesn't he, the vet I mean?'

'Yes, very pleasant,' she replied and said no more.

As they drove up the track leading to the Holiday Park, Jack looked across the field towards Taz's house and thought he saw the dog, sitting, looking back towards him. 'Let me out here please Mum,' he said, 'I won't be long, I dropped something out of my jacket pocket, when I was carrying the kitten.' He hadn't really dropped anything, he just wanted to go and tell Taz what had happened; he was wracking his brains to say what he'd dropped, she was bound to ask. But Mum just said, 'Ok love, don't be too long, I expect you could do with a drink now, I know I'm ready for a cup of tea.'

Once out of the car, Jack raced across the field, calling for Taz who came running to meet him, then turned away into the woods again.

'You like it in here as much as I do, don't you boy?' said Jack when he caught up with the dog. He threw himself down on the path and patted the ground beside him Taz came and sat too, staring at Jack with his blue and brown eyes, a sort of doggy grin on his face. Jack ruffled Taz's neck and told him about the kitten and what he was going to do tomorrow. He also said he hoped he had enough money to pay the vet bills and the damaged car. Taz licked his hand and snuffled Jack's ear, as if to say, 'Don't worry.'

'I wonder if you've met Mark Carter, the vet?' said Jack looking at Taz, who immediately jumped up, shook his head and bounded off towards his home. Jack laughed, 'I'm guessing you don't like going to the vet, oh well see you tomorrow Taz,' and off he went back to the caravan.

Chapter 7

Jack was up earlier than usual the next morning and was busily filling his pockets with biscuits, when his mother crept up behind him and said, 'That's not a very good breakfast, young man.'

Jack leapt about six feet in the air and guiltily replied, 'I'm um going to see if there's any ducks on the pond.' She gave him a puzzled look, so he hastily added, 'The one on the field, you know, at the end of the road that leads here.' He turned away flushing at the little white lie, but then he could go by the pond on the way to Taz's house.

'Ok, but you'd be better off taking some bread, I'll make breakfast while you're gone, about half an hour, alright?'

Jack grabbed some crusts from the bread bin and rushed off before she could mention the biscuits again. It looked as though it was going to be another fine day, he'd planned to spend a little time playing with Taz before going to meet up with Mark, the vet again, perhaps he'd find the dog first and they could both go to the pond together. It was still quite early and he saw hardly any people about.

Whistling in a, what he thought was a 'come here dog' sort of way, Jack was pleased to see Taz come bounding over towards him. Kneeling down and ruffling the dog around his ears and neck, Jack got a biscuit out of his pocket and held it out to Taz, who didn't even sniff at it before he gobbled it down. They then shared another one and with the dog at his heels Jack headed towards the pond. There was a thick clump of bulrushes in the middle and as they got closer Jack saw two coots, or maybe they were moorhens, swim swiftly towards them, to hide from the boy and dog. While he threw bread into the pond, Taz sat and watched, his strange eyes flickering between Jack's pocket, his hand and the ripples on the water. The water birds stayed hidden, so Jack moved away and lay down, pulling Taz close to him. 'Let's wait and see if the birds come out,' he said. The two lay close and shared more biscuits and eventually a small black water bird came out from its hiding place and swam around after the bread. Jack felt Taz tense up beside him as though he was going to jump in and chase the bird, but the boy kept his hand on the furry neck. After a while the other bird appeared and when all the bread seemed to have been eaten, they swam away to another part of the pond.

'That's it Taz,' said Jack as he stood up, 'I'm going for my breakfast now, so I might see you later.' Patting the dog again and feeding him the last bits of biscuit, he pointed towards Taz's house and said, 'Home boy, see you soon.' Taz gave Jack's hand one more lick then ran off towards his garden, and the boy walked quickly back to the caravan, hoping that Mum had cooked eggs on toast for breakfast.

Chapter 8

After eating and helping to clear up, Jack said he wanted to draw a poster, to advertise the 'found' kitten. Luckily, being a schoolteacher, she had plenty of plain paper and colouring things with her.

'Crayons are probably best,' she said, 'they stand out more than pencils and last longer than felt tips.'

After about an hour, Jack held up his finished masterpiece for inspection.

'That's really good Jack, you're quite an artist,' his mother smiled, 'the kitten picture is very realistic.' Proudly Jack picked up his poster and said he'd take it to the office right away, so that they could be off to the vets, as soon as he came back.

'I think we'll have time for a mid morning drink before we go,' said Mum, 'we don't want to be there too early.'

'Whatever,' sighed Jack and off he went.

At the office, Sheila the receptionist admired Jack's poster and gave him a pin to stick it on the notice board. Jack thanked her and put the poster up under the one for the painting competition, if he was as good as his Mum had said, he might win a prize for it even though he wouldn't be here, the judging would be at the end of the season party.

Just before 12 o' clock, they arrived back at the vets and Jack jumped out the car and ran into the waiting room. The same lady was behind the desk as the day before and Jack read her nametag. It said, 'Lynn Olds, Veterinary Nurse.'

He said, 'Hello,' just as his mother came in.

Lynn said, 'Mr. Carter said you can park round the back, if you like.'

'Thanks,' smiled Lisa and went out again. 'Meet me round there', she said to Jack

Jack walked round and saw a large fenced off grassy area, next to a shed. There were a few vehicles including Mr. Carter's Land Rover which had been cleaned. Jack inspected the bumper and was thankful to see there was no trace of his shopping trolley incident. Now the mud had been cleaned off he could read the words 'Veterinary Surgeon,' on the spare wheel cover. Suddenly a frenzied barking arose from inside the car and a black and white dog jumped up at the rear window. 'Aaagghhh,' yelled Jack jumping backwards away from the car in surprise and into the arms of Mark Carter, who managed to hang on to the cat basket he was carrying. 'Wow,' said Jack, 'what's his name, is he vicious?

'Her name is Nell and no she's not,' laughed Mark. 'She's just protecting my car, did she make you jump?'

'No, not at all,' mumbled the boy and immediately changed the subject, by looking into the cat basket. 'Hello Tam,' he murmured, wiggling his fingers through the mesh door 'how are you today?' The little kitten, seeing Jack's fingers, patted them with a soft paw, bringing a happy grin to the boy's face.

Mark explained that Tam was well on the mend, now he was warm, dry and full of food and he would probably be found a good home before long.

Seeing Jack's wistful face, his mother piped up, 'but not with us, I can see what you're thinking young man.'

Once Mark had introduced them both to Nell, Jack asked if he could sit with her in the back, where he kept up a lot of silly chatter and stroked her constantly. Whenever he stopped she raised a paw and pushed him on the arm, and tried to wriggle her head under his hand.

'Why does she do that, will she get cross with me if I stop stroking her?' he asked Mark.

'She likes the attention and will let you do that all day, given the chance,' replied the vet. 'Just tell her, "no more" and fold your arms, she'll settle down again.'

Jack wanted to ask Mark about Taz, but in a roundabout sort of way, so Mum wouldn't get suspicious, so he said, 'Is Nell a collie?'

'She's a collie crossed with a retriever,' said Mark.

'What colour are collies?' Jack carried on.

'Depends on the breed, there are all sorts, I'll show you a dog book I have back at the surgery, if you like?'

Jack's mother frowned and said, 'Don't let him disturb you Mark, this trip you're taking us on is a real treat, you don't have to spend more time with him and his questions.'

Mark smiled at her and said, 'It's a pleasure to have the company of such nice people, on a trip like this.' Now it was her turn to blush and she looked out of the window.

After a short time, they turned into the driveway of a large bungalow and Jack could see a huge cat, sunning itself on an indoor window ledge.

'Just take it easy Jack,' Mum said sternly, 'Wait and see what Mark wants us to do, we don't want to frighten anyone or anything.'

'It's ok Lisa, Jackie the owner is a Grandmother to two boys about Jack's age, she's used to youngsters.'

'Even so I don't want him letting me down,' she said and watched as Jack climbed out of the car, thoughtfully winding down the window so Nell could have some fresh air.

'Thanks son,' said Mark, 'here you carry Tam,' and he passed the basket to the boy.

Jackie was a smiley faced plumpish lady who greeted them all like old friends. 'Nice of you to bring me some new customers,' she said to Mark, looking from him to Lisa with a sparkle in her eyes.

'We've brought you a kitten, his name is Tam and I found him in the woods, nearly dead,' gabbled Jack holding up the basket.

Jackie peered in and saw Tam, curled up asleep, 'How sweet,' she said, 'let's get him out.' Jack carefully put the basket down and opened the door, Jackie, reached in and gently picked up the soft little bundle. She held him against her cheek, crooning softly to him. He opened his eyes, gave a great yawn and licked her face. 'Here Jack, you take him while I show you around,' she said and put Tam in the boy's arms.

For the next half-hour they wandered around the huge garden. Jack saw cats, guinea pigs, a few rabbits and a bird aviary he wanted to stay forever.

He was stroking and murmuring to Tam, when suddenly the little body twisted in his arms and jumped down. 'Oh no,' shouted Jack and went to run forward, but Mark grabbed his arm and stopped him,

'Look,' he said. They all stood still and watched in amazement as Tam ran up to a large ginger cat, which was washing its face with a paw. He jumped on the big cat's back then rolled down to the floor in front of it then he lay on his back and waved his tiny paws in the air, trying to reach the ginger face.

'Well I never,' said Jackie, 'that's Molly she's been here about two weeks, just turned up one day, do you think they know each other?'

PART 1   JACK

'They do now,' said Lisa and they all laughed.

Much later, when Jack was curled up in his bunk, he thought about the day and how much he'd enjoyed it. Mark and Nell were fun to be with. On the way back from Jackie's, they'd stopped at a pub for lunch, and then taken Nell for a walk. Mark had talked about all sorts of interesting things to do with his work. Mum had seemed relaxed and happy and he vaguely remembered her telling Mark about her job and Dad's accident; and the way Mark had patted her shoulder in a comforting gesture. Best of all, Mark had asked Jack if he'd like to come and visit a sick horse, later in the week, silly question, of course he would. Jack fell asleep.

Chapter 9

The rest of their holiday went far too quickly. Jack managed to visit Taz most days, if only for a little while. His mum and he had a few more outings with Mark and Nell, and Jack had read the dog book that Mark had lent him. Grey and white collies were often called 'Blue Merles' and were well known for having two different coloured eyes. When Jack had asked Mark if he knew any locally, the vet said he remembered one but he thought the owner had moved away.

One morning, Jack went to meet up with Taz and feed the ducks again, he was feeling a bit sad because their holiday was coming to an end. He sat by the pond with the dog at his side. He stroked and talked to him about Mark and Nell and he told Taz how much he loved him and didn't want to go home. The dog just looked at him, cocked his head from one side to the other and occasionally, reached out a paw to tap the boy's arm, when the stroking stopped. Suddenly Taz jumped up and ran off towards his home, Jack was about to follow, when he heard his Mum calling him, from the car. Cross at being disturbed, he slouched over to the driver's window and said, 'what?'

Ignoring his sullen face, Lisa said, 'Mark's just 'phoned, he wants to know if you want to go and see Tam again, I can drop you off at the surgery and go on to town.'

'Yes please,' shouted Jack, all smiles again, 'aren't you coming too?'

'I'm going to look for a 'thank you,' present for Mark, he's been so good to us this holiday,' replied his mother.

'Will you miss him when we go home, I will?' said the boy.

She didn't answer that, just told him to jump in the car.

He had a lovely morning with Mark at Jackie's place, Tam and Molly the older cat, were inseparable and Jackie said either they'd have to be adopted together, or she would keep them.

'I wish I could see them again,' sighed Jack to no one in particular. He didn't see the look that passed between the vet and Jackie.

On the way back, Mark asked Jack if he'd enjoyed his holiday,

'Best ever,' the boy answered, then he blurted out, 'I'll miss all this, you and Nell and Jackie, I think I'll be a vet or have a rescue home, when I'm older.'

Mark, smiled and said, 'I'll miss you too Jack and your mum.'

The boy looked surprised and mumbled something then said, 'We've gone past your place.'

'I agreed to take you back to the caravan, Lisa's invited me to lunch,' Mark grinned, and they both relaxed again, soppy talk out of the way.

As it was a nice day, they ate outside and when his mother went back into the caravan to get more drinks, she asked Jack to come and help her. Once inside she handed Jack a bag of dog treats and a framed picture of Nell. 'They're thank you presents,' she said, 'I took the picture on my 'phone when we all had lunch at the pub and I bought the frame this morning

'Wow,' said Jack, I wish I had one of Nell . . . and Mark,' he added. His mother just smiled.

Mark was so pleased with his present he gave Jack a hug and asked him if he was allowed to hug Lisa.

'Of course, she won't mind, she likes hugs,' said the boy opening the treats for Nell, who was lying under the picnic table, tail wagging at the rustling bag.

Later after Mark had gone back for evening surgery, Jack wandered over to the office. His poster was still up and on an impulse he decided to tell Sylvia a little white lie. 'I'm taking it down; he has a happy new home with a lady called Jackie and a big cat called Molly.'

Sylvia told him that no one had said they'd lost a kitten, but now if anyone asked, she'd say the kitten had gone to a new home. 'A lot of people liked your picture though Jack,' she said. 'You should just leave the kitten part for the competition.'

That's a good idea thought Jack as he left the office and hands in pockets, he felt the dog chew he'd pinched from Nell's bag. She won't mind he thought and ran off to find Taz.

Chapter 10

It was their last day of holiday and they had to leave the caravan by ten o' clock the following morning. Both Jack and Lisa were quiet but tried to appear happy to each other. They intended to have a great last day and had made a picnic, to take to the river, where they were going to hire a rowing boat as a special 'end of holiday' outing. Jack had a go at rowing, but wasn't very good, so his mum took over and they tied up at a pontoon, on the other side of the river to have lunch. While they were eating, Mum suddenly stopped stood up and pointed across the river, 'Look there, is that Nell?' she asked. Jack looked up and saw Taz running along the riverbank, looking over at him, before he turned away and ran off into some trees.

'No, wrong colour,' was all he replied and before either could say anything else, Lisa's 'phone rang.

Jack wondered what Taz was doing, he still didn't want Mum to know about the dog, who'd luckily run out of sight. He felt a little jolt in his tummy and a lump in his throat, he felt sad. He was really happy being here, he'd had a fabulous holiday and Mark reminded him of how his dad had been. He'd been a gamekeeper and knew all about woods and wildlife, a real outdoors person, which had rubbed off on Jack. Dad had always talked about all sorts of interesting stuff and tried out new things, Jack really missed him. Mark had briefly filled that gap, during this holiday.

Gazing across the water and still deep in thought, Jack was suddenly brought back by Mum, shaking his arm and saying,

'Hey dreamer, that was Mark, he wants us to have dinner together this evening. if you'd like to, as it's our last night. That's if you'd like to, as it's our last night.'

'I do if you do mum,' said Jack with a big grin, feeling happy again.

'Yes,' she replied, 'I really do.'

The rest of the afternoon passed very quickly and after returning the boat, they went back to their caravan, to finish packing. While she did the cleaning up, Jack wandered off to say goodbye to Taz and to tell him that he'd come and see him again, next time they came here. He'd make sure that they came here again. He remembered the fuss he'd made two weeks ago, when he didn't want to come. I must've been nuts, he thought.

Jack and Taz played together for a while, both chasing the sticks that Jack threw, then playing tug of war with them. Eventually he threw himself down on the leaves and called Taz over. Putting his arms around the soft body he hugged him tight and with tears in his eyes, he said, 'I gotta go Taz, but I'll be back another day.' The dog licked his face and wriggled out of the boy's arms, then sat and looked at him with his strange eyes and his doggy grin, then with a final lick of Jack's hand he ran off, back towards his house.

By the time Jack got back to the caravan, he'd cheered up at the thought of dinner with Mark and he hoped Nell would be there too. He quickly washed his hands and face, put on clean jeans and jumper, at Mum's insistence and waited impatiently for Mark to come and collect them.

Dinner was great fun, with his favourite food and lots of laughs but unfortunately Nell had to wait in the car. Dogs weren't allowed in this restaurant.

'She doesn't mind it's her second home,' Mark explained, 'she knows I'll be going back to it, sooner than I'll go back to the house.'

'Where is your house?' asked Jack.

'It's the surgery,' Mark answered, 'upstairs is my living area, and I'm there overnight for the animals that have to stay. I can get to them quickly then, if there's an emergency.'

All three of them talked about everything, Mark's and Mum's work, Jack's school and what he liked to do. He preferred being outdoors than inside watching TV or playing on computers, unless it was wet. The time flew by. Eventually they fell silent at the same time, all thinking that this was their last time together, when Mark suddenly announced he had something to say. He glanced at Mum, who looked as though she were about to cry. He said, 'I've become very fond of you guys, I want to stay in touch and see you again. This place has an End of Season Party in August before they close for the season. I usually get asked to come and help out in some way.'

'Oh wow, yes please,' shouted Jack, 'I'll be able to see Taz again as well.' He jumped up and flung his arms around Mark's neck.

'Don't you mean Tam?' said Mum absently as she reached over and grabbed one of Mark's hands, 'There's nothing I'd like more Mark,' she said, a huge smile on her face. And so saying she fumbled in her bag for her 'phone, summoned their waiter and showed him how to take a picture. Mark grabbed Jack onto his knee, pulled Lisa closer with his spare arm and they all shouted 'CHEESE' as their picture was captured onto Lisa's 'phone.

Chapter 11

Very early the next morning, Jack scrabbled about in his Mum's

Homework box and found paper and colouring pencils. He set to work and after about an hour, he'd finished what he was doing. He was just putting the stuff away as Lisa woke up. 'I'll put the kettle on,' said Jack to distract her from asking what he was up to, 'then I'm going to the office, to see if anyone's asked about Tam.'

'Why don't you wait until we hand the keys in?' said his mother, sleepily.

'Too many people about, I won't get a chance to talk to Sylvia,' Jack quickly replied and rushed out, his jumper making a strange rustling sound over his tummy.

By 9.30, Jack and Lisa were all packed up and ready to go. He got his bag and took it out to the car while Lisa double checked, that they hadn't left anything behind, then she came out, locked the door and gave him the key. 'Hand this in at the office please love,' she said, 'I'll meet you outside there in a minute.'

He ran off, disappointed that they were leaving now, but happy to know that they'd be back in a few weeks. Mum had said that they would stop off at Mark's surgery on the way, to say a last goodbye to him and Nell and arrange when to 'phone each other. Jack had to remember to tell Mark to tell Jackie that Tam was all hers; no one would be claiming the kitten now. He couldn't wait till the party in August.

Finally they were on their way and as the car drove slowly through the park gates and out onto the track, Jack glanced across his Mum to look out of her window, in the distance he saw a white fluffy tail, disappearing into the trees. 'See you soon Taz,' he said inside his head. 'See you soon.'

PART 2

KATIE

Chapter 12

Katie Lowther wasn't happy as she walked home from school with her younger brother. Apart from being teased again for being overweight, it was the first Friday of May so Monday was a Bank Holiday. Firstly, her mum was going away for a month, to Scotland of all places, to look after Grandma, who was recovering from a leg operation and needed help. Secondly, Katie didn't like spending more time than she had to with her two brothers, eight year old Josh and fourteen year old Sam. Like their dad they were very fit and sporty. Thirdly and worst of all, it meant that they had to spend most weekends now at the holiday park, where they had their own big caravan. She hated these weekends, there was always so much stuff going on that involved sports and the wretched swimming pool would now be open. Although she could swim a bit, her parents wanted her to become better at it.

Katie was twelve and from September would be going to the local pool once a week with her school class. She was dreading it, last time she'd put her swimsuit on it was too tight, even though it was adult size, and she knew she was fatter now. Why did she have to go to the only High School in the County that still included swimming in it's Games Lessons? Mum had said she'd get her a new suit, but hadn't got round to it yet, because of worrying about Grandma. Other kids at school teased her anyway, never mind if she was in a swimsuit!

Katie's Mum and Dad kept telling her that as she grew taller all her 'puppy fat' would spread out with her, but she wasn't growing taller quickly enough, or so she thought. Sometimes Josh would ask her to play ball with him, or mess about on the play equipment in their garden, but she'd always give up after a short while, complaining she was too hot, too cold, too tired, but never too fat.

She didn't have a best friend, mainly because she thought people wouldn't like to be seen with a fat person and she was quite shy. The other kids in her class were used to her now, so she didn't get teased so much, but going to the caravan meant there'd be new families there on holiday. There were also the families like hers, who had their own caravans with kids she'd been teased by before.

When they got home, their mother was in the kitchen writing one of her endless lists. 'Hi guys,' she smiled, 'had a good day, looking forward to the weekend?'

'No . . . , Yes . . . ,' Katie and Josh said together. Josh immediately dived into the fridge for a snack, while Mum looked at Katie and said, 'What's up love?'

'Can't I go with you to Grandma's Mum; I don't want to go to the caravan and have to play outside all the time with the others?'

'We've talked about this, you still have school to go to and the weekends at the holiday park will be fun, if you cheer up and let them be,' said their mother. 'Look I'm making a list of things to do, while I'm away, you're the boss of the house now, you'll have to make sure these three lazy boys do as *you* tell them,' she carried on, attempting to cheer Katie up and make her realise how important she was.

'Dad's not a boy and Sam won't listen to me,' she answered sulkily and went up to her room where she had a secret stash of chocolate bars and crisps. She'd have to hide some in her weekend bag; Dad wouldn't let her eat what he called 'rubbish.' She also hid the horrible tight swimsuit behind some books, before Mum came to check and help her pack. She'd say she hadn't seen it since last summer.

Chapter 13

By eleven o' clock the following morning, Katie, her brothers and Dad, were sorting out their caravan. They'd left early and dropped Mum at the airport on the way. Katie tried to be brave and not tearful, she'd miss her mother, but it was only for four weeks and she was already thinking about making a welcome home present, for when she got back. Josh cried a bit, but Katie put her arm round him in the car and asked him to help her with the surprise present, so he was soon carried away with his big ideas and then what they were going to do this weekend, that he cheered up.

While Dad and the boys finished unpacking the car Katie went to the holiday camp office, to let them know they'd arrived. She smiled shyly at Sylvia, who she remembered from past years and who said, 'Hi Katie, you've grown since I last saw you.'

Katie immediately looked away, thinking Sylvia meant she'd grown fatter and said over her shoulder, 'You should see Sam, he's nearly as big as Dad now,' and she wandered over to the notice board, to check out what she might be forced into over the next few weekends. Oh no, she thought, as she read about a fun swimming gala. She also saw a poster for a two mile Dawn Chorus walk followed by breakfast at a pub. A four o' clock in the morning start wasn't very appealing, but breakfast was, she'd think about that. There was also a painting competition and a Fun Run coming up. Katie couldn't understand why the word Fun kept cropping up in sporting events.

Wandering back to the caravan, she found Dad and Josh getting ready to go to the supermarket, while Sam wanted to check out who was at the pool. Not wanting to join in either activity, Katie said she'd stay and tidy up a bit, but really she wanted to delve into her secret snack supply, while they were all out of the way.

'Dad, did you pack any of our favourite DVD's?' she asked her father.

'No love, I thought that as it's supposed to be fine weather this weekend, we'd make the most of being outside. You've all had too much time indoors over the winter. A bit of fresh air and exercise will do us all good'.

'You mean me, Katie thought and went off to her room. She didn't hear dad sigh as he watched her walk away.

When her family had left, she slumped down on one of the couches and switched the TV on. Unfortunately the only channel she could get a clear picture on had a bunch of old people talking about world money markets. Boring thought Katie and went back to her room to find her ipod. Plugging the music into her ears, she rummaged in her bag and chose two packets of crisps and three chocolate biscuit bars. Stuffing them into her fold up backpack, she took a small bottle of fizzy cola from the kitchen and left the caravan. She locked it and left the key in the usual hiding place, under the spare gas bottle. Katie didn't want to eat her snacks in the caravan, someone would be bound to smell the crisps, or find the empty wrappers, so she decided to go to the picnic area, the other side of the park.

On her way there she stopped by the pool to let Sam know she was out. He'd already met up with three other youngsters, a girl and two boys. She thought she recognised them from last year, but was too shy and self-conscious to say hello. Katie quickly spoke to her brother and went on her way again. As she turned away she heard the girl say, 'That's never your sister Sam, how come she's so fat?'

Mortified, Katie felt her cheeks go hot and she stumbled on, she rammed the earplugs back into her ears, so she couldn't hear Sam's reply or any of the usual laughter, which usually followed these comments. Nor did she hear one of the other boys' say, 'Don't be so mean.' Not stopping at the picnic area now, Katie carried on and didn't slow down, until she reached the woods, bordering the park. Hot and sweating, from walking so fast, she sank down under a tree and brushing tears from her eyes, she opened her backpack and pulled out her drink and a packet of crisps.

Chapter 14

She finished one packet and opened the other, her head was hanging as she nodded in time to the music. Her eyes were closed while she ate and just as the song she was listening to came to its, Katie heard a loud rustling and crackling, from behind her. Pulling the ear plugs out she turned and gasped as a grey and white dog appeared from the undergrowth behind her tree and came and lay itself, on its tummy in front of her. Katie sat frozen to the spot, she was scared of dogs, and they could run faster than she could. Poor Katie heard a sort of mewling sound and realised it was coming from her open mouth. She didn't know what to do; she clamped her lips shut, closed her eyes and willed the dog to go away. 'Shoo, shoo, shoo,' she whimpered and cautiously opened one eye. The dog just sat and looked at her, its tongue was hanging out and it was panting. It looked as though it was smiling. Dog and girl stared at each other and Katie noticed it had one brown eye and one blue. She'd never seen anything like that before. Gradually she relaxed and decided she'd try and stand up and walk away, but being so big, she found it difficult to stand up slowly and keep the dog in sight at the same time. As soon as she moved on to her hands and knees, the dog sat up, causing her to gasp with fear. As if it understood her distress the dog lay down again. She managed to get one foot to the ground and bracing one hand against the tree, she stood up, her legs were trembling and the open bag of crisps in her lap fell to the floor. They both stared at the scattered snacks on the ground then the dog stretched its head forward along its front paws. The black nose twitched as it breathed in the smell of beef flavouring. Unable to reach, it shuffled forward on its tummy until it could just stretch out its tongue to lick up the crisp. But it stopped as Katie watched, fascinated, and looked at her as though to say, 'can I have one?'

'Go on,' she said, 'eat it up,' and at the sound of her voice the dog did and crunched it with open mouth. If I did that, thought the girl, Mum would tell me off for eating with my mouth open, and despite her fear, she allowed herself a small smile.

Licking its lips, the dog sat up again, but kept staring at the other crisps. Katie told herself that it was hungry and wasn't going to attack her, so she sat down again and stretched her hand out and picked one up. As she leaned forwards, the dog shied away a bit, but Katie held it out in her fingers, keeping her hand very still. Slowly the dog stretched forward and gently took the snack from the girl's fingers. Feeling braver, Katie did it again and again, until there was nothing left apart from the scent on the floor and her hand. Cautiously she held that out and equally tentatively the dog licked her fingers clean. She felt a burst of happiness, she had just about conquered one of her fears. Dogs! Her eyes brightened with tears. Katie carried on holding out her hand, but the dog just looked at her, but its tail swept backwards and forwards across the ground, causing dead leaves and dust to jump into the air. Trying something else, she patted her hand on the ground beside her and softly said, 'come on then.' It lay down again and shuffled over then sat beside her. She murmured quietly and it rested its head on one of her plump legs. For the first time in a long while Katie felt really happy, she'd made a friend.

Chapter 15

She didn't know how much later it was, when she made a move to get up and go back to the caravan. It was cooler now, so hopefully Sam and the other kids would have left the pool area, and wouldn't be there to tease her again. As she struggled to her feet, the dog jumped up and started running off. 'Don't go,' she called out and it stopped. It turned and looked at her, gave a sort of grin, ran back, licked her hand, then rushed off into the woods. By the time Katie had picked up her bag and turned to follow, it had gone, but it had left her with a warm feeling inside, she knew she'd meet it again.

Back at the caravan, her brothers and Dad were just sitting down to fish and chips, presumably from the local takeaway.

'Hi stranger,' Dad smiled, 'had a nice afternoon, grab a plate?'

Seeing Sam's smirking face, Katie just helped herself to some fish and replied, 'Yes thanks, I met up with a new friend.'

'Yeah sure,' said Sam, 'what's their name then?'

Oh, gosh, thought Katie, I didn't look for a collar or nametag. So quickly picturing the dog in her mind, she said, 'Er, Collie.'

Dad mis-heard her, 'Carly,' that's a nice name, will we get to meet her?'

'Dunno, maybe,' his daughter replied, her face reddening. She didn't want to share her newfound friend, especially as it was a dog, so to change the subject she said. 'I'm not so hungry Dad I took some stuff with me.' The three of them looked at her in surprise, they'd never known Katie to refuse food. The she added, 'Who's doing what tomorrow?'

After supper, Sam wandered off to meet up with his friends again, but he had to be back before dark, Dad sat on the sofa reading the daily paper and Katie helped Josh, draw some pictures which he could stick things to, as present for Mum.

'You're a good drawer Katie,' he said.

'Artist, not drawer, that's a bit of furniture,' she laughed and immediately drew a picture of a drawer with arms and legs and a smiley face. Josh giggled and Dad came and looked over their shoulders at the pictures,

'You are good love,' he said patting her on the shoulder, 'well done.'

Just then Sam came back in and said 'Katie's got to be good at something apart from eating.'

The laughter stopped, Katie hung her head, so her hair covered her face and no one could see the tears in her eyes. Josh just turned and glared at his older brother and Dad quietly said, 'Katie has many good qualities, particularly being nice to people, unlike someone not far from here.'

Sam shrugged, mumbled, 'Sorry, sis' and went to his bedroom.

Behind her curtain of hair, Katie had a sudden image of two strange eyes and a doggy grin. Sitting up straight again, she looked at Josh, smiled and said, 'What shall we draw now?'

'A beach,' shouted the young boy, 'we can find some shells tomorrow, down at the shore, and then stick them on a picture for Mum.'

'That's a good idea Josh, mum loves the beach too.'

With peace restored, the evening passed quickly and they were all happier when they went off to their beds.

Chapter 16

Katie woke early; she lay and listened, but didn't think anyone else was up yet. She sat up and looked out of her window; the sky was clear and blue so it would probably be a nice day. Dad and the boys were going swimming later and they didn't know yet that she hadn't brought her swimsuit with her. She'd have the chance to go out without them and try to find the dog again. Maybe she could get it to go to the shore with her and she could collect some shells for Josh. She was actually looking forward to doing this, a feeling she hadn't had for a long time, Katie got up and set about getting breakfast ready.

When they were all sittingt around the table later, Dad said, 'Is that all you're having Katie?' he looked at her empty cereal bowl.

'Um yes, I was up way before you guys, I already had something else,' she said untruthfully. The fact was she was so excited about seeing the dog again, she wasn't hungry.

'Hmm, ok,' said Dad.

'Don't all look at me like that,' snapped the girl and stomped off to start washing up.

The boys went off to their room to get their swimming stuff and Dad picked up a tea towel to dry up the dishes.

'I'll do it, you go, I'll catch up later,' Katie said.

'Sure'

'Yes.'

'You *will* come over to the pool.'

'Yes Dad,' she sighed 'see you there.'

Once they'd all gone, Katie grabbed her trusty backpack, filled it with a couple of ham sandwiches, some bags of crisps, chocolate bars an apple and a banana and two bottles of water.

Water! she thought no more fizzy drinks for me I doubt if dogs like fizz, and off she went towards the pool.

Trying to sneak around without being seen was impossible, as there were lots of families already there. Squeezing her large body between sun beds was embarrassing and she got several stern looks from adults and sniggers from children. Finding her father, she whispered, 'I can't find my swimsuit, is it ok if I go find Carly?'

Dad gave her a half smile and said, 'Of course you can, have fun, will you be back for lunch?'

'Depends what we do, we may go to the shore, but I'll be very careful and certainly be back for supper,' and before her father could reply, she walked away towards the woods.

Finding the same spot as the day before, Katie sat down and took a bag of crisps from her bag. As she was rattling the packet, she heard a rustling noise and turning saw the dog emerge from some undergrowth behind the trees. It came straight over and sat on hind legs in front of her, looking first to her face, then the bag in her hands. Katie laughed and took her time opening the packet and taking a crisp out, she pretended she was going to put it in her mouth. The dog stretched his head forward and as it did so, she caught sight of a chain around its furry neck. Reaching forward she gave the dog the crisp and as it was crunched up, she gently felt for the collar. Pulling it round she found a worn silver coloured disc with a rather faded TAZ stamped on one side. 'Taz,' breathed Katie, 'nice name, better than Carly, you must be a boy, my first boyfriend.' She laughed aloud while Taz just looked at her, then at the food again.

A bag of crisps and some ham sandwiches later, Katie decided the dog had, had enough to eat and that he needed a walk. It didn't even enter her head that she didn't like walking. They strolled along together and sometimes, Taz broke into a run, making Katie speed up to follow him. She chatted all the while, and told him about her unhappy, fat life. He was a good listener and every so often he'd come up and lick her hand.

The morning passed into afternoon and apart from sitting down to share a bottle of water and a banana, the two companions wandered on.

Katie was just telling Taz about Mum's picture, when she stopped, gasped and said, 'Shells, I've got to get some for Josh, oh no, which way to the shore?' As she turned this way and that, seeing nothing but trees and undergrowth, she suddenly realised that they were nearly back where they'd started from and she knew how to get to the river from there. 'Come on Taz, this way,' she said, and off she went at a brisk walk. Before long, they'd reached the sign that said, 'To the shore.' Katie followed the path and as it was downhill, she broke into a slow run. Taz raced ahead of her and disappeared around a bend, he'd probably wait for her she thought.

The drop down on to the river beach was quite steep, though not too high and Katie lost her footing at the last minute and ended up rolling onto the sand.

'Wondered where you'd got to,' said a voice and looking up she saw Dad and Josh, already there.

'Oh hi,' muttered Katie as Dad held out his hand and helped her to her feet,' I was, um, just wondering where you were,' she was glancing around looking for the dog, but couldn't see him.

'Did you find Carly?'

'Er yeah we had fun, just chatting, y'know, getting to know each other.'

'Good for you, you've actually got a bit of colour in your cheeks, this new friend of yours is doing you some good already,' Dad added.

'Hey Josh,' got any shells yet?' Katie turned to her little brother, once again changing the subject.

The time passed, Katie was a bit distracted, as she tried to keep up a conversation with Dad and Josh, while all the time wondering if Taz would come back. She didn't want him to he was her special friend.

She didn't see him again, but as they wandered back to the campsite. Josh suddenly said,

'Hey look at that dog,' he pointed away in the distance,

'Where, what did it look like?' his sister asked him,

'A dog,' laughed the youngster.

After a supper of sausages and mash, Katie only had two sausages, she sneaked her third one into her pocket to give to Taz the next day, Dad and Sam watched TV while Katie and Josh sorted through the load of shells they'd collected.

'We've got hundreds,' said Josh, 'What shall we do with them all?'

'We can bring some paint next weekend and paint some,' said Katie.

'Take some home and I'll find time to make holes in them,' added Dad, 'then you can thread them on string or something, and make a hanging mobile.'

Before long, Sam also joined in the conversation with ideas of what to do with the shells and the four of them spent a happy family evening, something Katie hadn't enjoyed for a long time. She went to bed with a smile on her face.

Chapter 17

After breakfast the next morning they all helped to pack up the stuff they were going to take back home, later in the afternoon. Katie volunteered to clean inside the caravan, while her dad and brothers went off to play ball. She could then clear the fridge of anything that wouldn't keep and go and find Taz.

'We'll meet up for lunch together,' said Dad, 'then if there's time, we might go on a mystery trip, before heading home.'

'Ugh!' said Sam.

'Great,' said Josh,

'Fine,' mumbled Katie, hoping it wouldn't be somewhere, packed with smart, thin girls.

As she passed the picnic area a bit later, a boy called out, 'Hi Sam's sister, is he coming swimming today?' Katie pretended not to hear, but the boy ran over and said, 'Hey, I'm Danny, what's your name?'

'Katie,' she said feeling her face go red, then, 'Sam's with my Dad and Josh, I think they're playing football.'

'Oh, ok, I'd rather swim,' replied Danny, 'see ya Katie,' and off he went again.

She couldn't believe it, a boy had spoken to her without teasing or name-calling, it made her feel good inside.

Finding Taz was easy, it was as though he knew she'd have something to eat for him and was waiting under the tree where they'd first met. Katie ruffled his furry neck and gave him her supper sausage. When she didn't get anything else out of her bag, he ran off along a different path.

PART 2   KATIE

Following him as fast as she could, they eventually reached the edge of the wood and came out onto a field. Taz ran towards the road and Katie realised where they were. Although she'd seen it often enough from the car, she'd never actually walked here they were near the pond. Taz ran ahead, to the pond's edge, causing a couple of water birds to flap across the water, their feet leaving a trail like a mini wave. He stood sniffing the air and looked towards the bulrushes. Breathless, Katie ran up and sat down beside him. It was peaceful and she could just see some water birds trying to hide in the reeds.

Quietly she opened her bag and took out a sandwich. Taz immediately sat down on his haunches looked at her, his nose almost in her hand. 'Back off Taz,' she whispered, 'you have to share today,' and so saying she broke all the crusts off the bread and gave the eager dog the rest of the sandwich. The rest she started throwing into the pond, but had to stop and grab Taz by the collar, 'You're not a duck,' she said laughing, 'any way, you just had some.'

As they watched, the water birds, stayed in their reeds, but suddenly, there were little plopping sounds on the surface of the pond as small grey fish with red tails came up after the food.

The two friends sat and watched and eventually one of the water birds came out to investigate, it was black with a red beak. Katie made a mental note to find out what sort of bird it was and what the fish were. After the sandwiches and the rest of the food had been eaten, mostly by Taz and the birds, Katie stood up and said, 'Time to go boy it's all gone.' Looking around, she thought she'd like to come back here again one day and said the same thing to the dog. She told him they were going home later, but would be back next weekend. He listened to her, put his

53

head under her hand so she could stroke him around the ears, then moved his head and licked her fingers. Bending down in front of him, Katie looked into his odd eyes and kissed him on the nose. "Let's go boy,' she said and started walking towards the track leading back to the holiday park. Taz however had a different idea and as Katie watched, he ran in the opposite direction towards a cottage in the distance. There he jumped over a fence and disappeared from view into the garden. So that must be where he lives, thought Katie, as she made her way back to the caravan.

Chapter 18

Katie was in trouble. When she'd cleared out the fridge earlier, she hadn't remembered to leave some stuff for lunch and now they all thought she'd scoffed the lot. Sam and Josh were having a go at her until Dad shouted, 'Enough, what's done is done, we'll have to eat out so we won't have time to go the Rescue Home for stray animals. Bring your stuff to the car, let's go.'

Sam and Josh both glared at their sister and she was so miserable, she didn't notice a furry face watching the car as they left the campsite, until Josh said 'Hey look, there's that dog again.'

'What dog?' his brother asked.

'One we saw at the beach, wish we had a dog.'

Dad just grunted. Katie turned to look out of the back window and saw Taz, sitting by the track, his tongue hanging out, grinning at her. She wiggled her fingers in a wave to him. Sam had also turned around from his seat in front, next to Dad, and saw what she did.

'Ha, mad as well as greedy,' he muttered. Dad just glared at his eldest son.

Katie's misery was now mixed with anger and inside her head she said, 'Just you wait, you lot, 'I'll show you.'

Chapter 19

Three weeks later, Katie, the boys and Dad were all looking forward to seeing Mum again. They'd all helped to tidy up the house and garden in her absence and were hoping that she'd join them at the caravan on Saturday afternoon. Katie was a bit nervous as she'd overheard her dad on the 'phone, telling Mum, that he was concerned about their daughter.

'She seems to be eating much more at weekends but she's losing weight,' he said.

Katie still hadn't told any of them about Taz and Dad had given up asking her about Carly, whenever she went off on her own. She'd have to think of something to stop them worrying.

The morning of Mum's return was bright and sunny and as usual Sam drifted off to swim and meet up with his friends. Dad and Josh went to the supermarket leaving Katie to put the finishing touches to the shell picture that Josh had made. When she'd finished she packed her bag with a few snacks left a note to say she'd be back by lunchtime and went off to find Taz. Thinking about him brought a smile to her face; they'd had some great times, the past few weekends. They'd chased each other along the beach and through the woods. Whenever Katie tried to hide from him, he soon found her, one time she'd even managed to climb up some low branches on an oak tree. Taz had made a big show of sniffing around the base of the tree, before he finally looked up and yelped at her.

Passing the picnic area and the pool, she caught sight of Sam chatting to the boy called Danny. She gave a sort of half wave as she passed them and Danny raised his hand in greeting and said something to Sam. They both stared at her then and thinking the worst, Katie hurried on by towards the woods.

The rest of the morning with Taz passed by in a flash and making her way back later, Katie came face to face with Danny.

'Hi Katie, Sam's already gone back to your caravan.' Then, without any warning, he grabbed her by the hand and pulled her towards the pool.

'Let me go, what are you doing?' yelled Katie, thinking he was going to throw her in, fully clothed.

'Don't worry, just look at that lovely blue water, waiting for you to come and swim with us,' Danny pointed at the sparkling water, grinned and let go of her hand. Heart thumping, Katie looked at him, then the pool and said, 'I can't swim.'

'Your brother said you can, but you won't, because you worry about how you look,' the boy continued. 'Well I think you look great and you have a pretty face, not like my freckled mug and big ears.'

Katie didn't know what to say, she wanted to tell him to leave her alone, but he didn't look as if he were teasing her. 'I'll think about it,' she whispered and turning away she added, 'You haven't got big ears' and carried on.

Chapter 20

Hearing laughter as she approached the caravan, Katie suddenly noticed Mum's car parked there. She broke into a run and burst in through the door. Her mother looked up in surprise as this mini whirlwind threw herself into her arms.

'Katie, you look fabulous, so tanned and you've lost weight.'

The girl smiled and squeezed harder, 'I've been exercising,' she said, hearing Sam snort in the background, 'Oh, Mum I've missed you, is Granny alright now?'

Dad interrupted, 'Let's get lunch ready and we can all sit down and catch up with everything.'

They had lunch outside it was great fun. The three children all chattered at once, telling mum funny stories about each other and their friends. After, Katie and Mum were left alone to do the washing up while Dad and the boys went to collect swimming and football gear.

Suddenly Mum said, 'You're looking really good love, Dad says you've made a new friend called Carly, am I going to get to meet her?'

Katie didn't know what to say she didn't like keeping things from her family, but Taz was her special friend and she still didn't want to share him. She was about to give Mum a sort of vague reply, when thankfully, (first time ever) Josh burst in, grabbed his Mum by the hand and said, 'Come on you two, you can do that later.'

Laughing they followed him to where he'd put Mum's present. Katie pretended she hadn't helped with it as Josh proudly produced his shell picture.

Unknown to Dad and Katie, Sam had found a huge shell, which he'd used as a centrepiece for a hanging mobile. He gave this to their mother. He'd painted the shells, in gold and silver *and* he'd put glitter on them, making them twinkle as they spun around.

'Wow Sam, I didn't know you were so artistic,' said Katie sarcastically. They all stared at her; it wasn't like her to make mean comments.

'Well I think you're all fantastic,' said their mother as she hugged each one of them in turn. Sam pulled away, his gift was enough, and he didn't have to be sloppy as well.

The rest of Saturday passed in a blur and Katie didn't have time alone with her mother for any more chats about Carly.

She was also a whole lot happier she told her mum that girls at school now invited her to things and asked her to sit with them at lunchtimes. She joined in talking about girl stuff, hair, nails, make—up, fashion and boys, things she'd never been interested in before.

'Guess what mum? I found my swimsuit and it's *too big.*'

'Good for you, love, I'll buy you a new one and you must promise not to hide it behind your books.'

They both laughed and hugged each other.

Chapter 21

The next few weeks went really quickly, both Katie and Sam had school exams and were happy to relax at the caravan at weekends. She took homework books with her and when she sneaked off to meet Taz, she took them with her and said she was revising in peace. She actually did that at school and spent her Taz time, playing chase, hide and seek and Frisbee with him. Whenever anyone mentioned Carly, she said things like, 'She's got to revise for her exams,' or 'she's not here this weekend.'

Luckily the rest of Katie's family seemed to accept this, as they always had other things to keep them occupied.

Chapter 22

Finally the school term was at an end and Katie was actually looking forward to a whole two weeks at their caravan, she hoped to have more time to spend with Taz. Unfortunately she didn't have as much as she'd planned. She became one of the kids who hung around the swimming pool.

She got to know Danny better and one day, he seemed very quiet, and unlike his usual joking self.

'What's up with you, Mr. Not Big Ears?' Katie laughed, giving him a gentle push.

Danny grabbed her hand and quickly looking around to make sure no one was watching, he blurted out, 'Katie will you come to the end of season party with me, in August?'

With no hesitation, Katie grinned and said, 'Of course I will.' Inside her heart was thumping she felt so happy, she jumped up, 'Back in a minute,' she yelled and ran off.

Taz came running as soon as she called to him. She threw her arms round his neck and told him that Danny had asked her out. 'It's all thanks to you Taz,' she said, while he wagged his tail and gave her his tongue-hanging grin. 'Got to go now, boy, see you soon,' she gave him another hug and ran back towards the pool, happy tears in her eyes. She stopped, turned and waved just in time to see his fluffy tail disappearing back into the trees.

Before the family left the park later that afternoon, as usual Katie took their key to the office. 'Here's the key Sylvia,' said Katie, 'and also this,' she handed over a large brown envelope, 'it's a secret, don't tell anyone, see you next weekend,' and off she went.

PART 3
LIAM

Chapter 23

'For goodness sake shut the window and sit down,' Liam's mother complained. 'If you knew how many horrible germs from dirty hands and faces have been on that window, you wouldn't go near it.' Ten year old Liam did as he was told, he wasn't going to sulk or whine, he was happy, he was on his way to stay with his gran and granddad for a week, he couldn't care less about germs, that was one of his mum's worries.

It was his school's summer half term week and every year Liam stayed with his grandparents so Mum and Dad could get away on their own. This year she was bringing him on the train and she fussed and fretted the whole time, worried that he was going to get some dreaded disease. At home, if he coughed or sneezed she rushed to get a thermometer, a jumper for him to put on, or another blanket to wrap him in and lay him on the sofa. She'd even convinced the doctor that he had something called asthma so he had an inhaler, he called it a puffer, in his pocket all the time.

'How much longer, Mum?' he asked, 'What's the name of the station, can I look out of the window, so I know when we get there?'

'About another 10 minutes, and no, just sit still and read or something,' she answered, handing him an antiseptic wipe. 'Clean your hands, there's a good boy.'

'But I need germs to keep me healthy,' sighed Liam, taking the small damp piece of paper and wiping his hands. Then in a moment of defiance, he quickly wiped a spot on the window and leaned his face against it, trying to look ahead to where they were going.

'Sit down Liam, behave,' snapped his mother.

Finally, the train pulled into the station and he jumped up, wanting to be the first one out of the stuffy carriage. His mum grabbed him by the hand to stop him and said, 'Just wait, we're still moving, get your bag, is your inhaler in your pocket?'

'Yes, yes,' he said getting a bit cross and breathless.

'You'd better have a puff now, you're breathing fast,' his mother looked concerned and let go of his hand. She moved to get his inhaler out of his pocket but by now the train had stopped and Liam pulled away, opened the door and burst out onto the platform. Ignoring his mother's voice he quickly glanced around and saw Granddad up ahead.

Granddad, I'm here.' He shrieked.

The old man turned and held his arms open as the small whirlwind hurled itself into them. 'Hello my boy, good to see you again,' he smiled, 'where's your mother?'

'Hi Dad,' Liam's Mum came panting up, carrying his backpack and a small suitcase. 'He shouldn't do that, he'll make himself ill.'

'Nonsense,' Granddad's eyes twinkled. 'You worry too much, Sue my dear,' said her father, then taking Liam's hand in one of his own and the suitcase in the other, he said, 'Come on, let's go and find Gran,' and they made their way to his car.

Despite his mother's concern, Liam was allowed to sit in the front with Granddad and bombarded him with questions. 'Did the acorn we planted grow? Is Gran still working at the holiday place with a swimming pool? Have you been back to the animal shelter to see Jackie and her pets?'

Granddad laughed and said, 'We've got a whole week to catch up on all that, but yes to all your questions.'

'I hope you won't let him overdo things and make himself ill,' said a worried voice from the back seat.

'Of course we won't,' he half turned towards his daughter and at the same time gave Liam a quick wink.

Chapter 24

After lunch, Granddad took Sue back to the station and Liam breathed a happy sigh. He did love his mum lots, but he was a big boy now and wished she didn't worry so much about him. He felt a little bit guilty that he didn't go with them to wave her off, but he wanted to stay with Gran, who always spoiled him and didn't fuss over him so much.

'Where's my oak tree Gran?' he said grabbing her hand and dragging her towards the back door.

'Hold on,' she said, 'I'll just put my shoes on. I think it's still in the pot you planted it in, but I'm not sure where Granddad's put it.' They soon found it, Liam was thrilled to see it was about as tall as his knees and he asked if they could plant it in the ground now.

'You'll have to ask Granddad, I don't know if we need another oak tree in the garden.'

'The garden's huge, big enough for a whole forest,' said Liam as he ran off to explore it. The woodpile was a great place to investigate, sometimes there were lizards in it and once they'd found a slow worm. The garage used to be a barn and was full of all sorts of interesting old tools and cobwebs. Liam didn't mind spiders, it made him feel tough when Mum asked him to get rid of them from indoors, and she was *scared* of them.

Gran came up behind him and asked him how he was feeling these days. When she'd asked him before, his mum had butted in and said he was still getting too breathless when he got excited. Thankfully no one had made any more comments about that.

'I'm fine Gran, really I am,' he said hoping she wasn't going to make him go and rest.

'Good,' she replied, ruffling his hair—which he hated, but didn't say anything. 'Sometimes I think your Mum worries too much.'

'When can we go to the Holiday Park, Gran? Is there anything happening soon that I can join in? Can I go in the swimming pool this time?' Liam asked eagerly.

'We'll see, depends if you behave yourself,' Gran answered, then laughed when Liam's face fell into a sulky expression. 'Of course you can silly, but not unless you get rid of that moody face,' Come and have a look at the holiday events list, we'll see if anything is on at the same time that I'm there at work.'

Granddad came back as they were looking at the 'Things to do' paper. Liam said he'd like to do the adventure walk the next day. 'What is it exactly?' he asked.

'Do you remember Jean, the lady I work with sometimes? Her son Peter and his girlfriend are school teachers; they take groups of children on walks through the woods and along the shore. They teach you all sorts of things about wildlife and such and have competitions for finding things.'

'What sort of things?' Liam interrupted.

'Dragons, huge snakes and monsters' shouted Granddad from behind, making him jump and squeal.

'Don't do that,' said Liam crossly. His grandparents laughed.

'Things like, different sorts of trees and birds, holes in the ground, you have to decide what lives in them, wildflowers, what you can find to eat, all sorts of stuff it's very interesting and fun,' said Gran. 'I've heard a lot of the children who've been, say they enjoyed it. They take a packed lunch and drinks and spend time in the woods and on the shore.'

'Hmm ok, will you go with me Granddad?'

'Don't be daft, I'm too old, but I'll introduce you to the others. There might be some other kids there that you've met before.'

Liam hoped not. Last year he'd been teased by other children for not being allowed to take part in things. That had been a day when his mum was there and made him stay close to her, with his books and Gameboy and wearing a stupid sun hat. Thinking about that he said in a small voice, 'I hope it's not sunny tomorrow, then I won't have to wear that stupid hat Mum packed for me.'

'Don't worry about that, you'll have a great time,' replied his grandfather. 'Gran's working in reception tomorrow morning so I'll take you over there to meet up with the others before you all leave for your walk, ok?'

'Alright,' said the boy and taking the old man by the hand, he said, 'Come on let's go and see where we can plant my oak tree.'

The two wandered outside leaving Gran with a smile on her face and Granddad with a puzzled frown.

Chapter 25

When he awoke the next morning, Liam's first thought was yippee I'm at Gran and Granddad's,' his second was, adventure walk and his third was, hope it's not sunny or I'll have to wear the silly hat.

It was still early and he wanted to see Gran before she went to work, so he quickly got dressed, had a quick wash with a damp flannel and went downstairs.

'Hi Gran, what's for breakfast, please don't say 'Wheaty Flakes.'

'Morning Liam, I bought 'Wheaty Flakes' especially, as I know how much you like them,' she said. Liam looked at her and was about to complain that he hated them, when he saw she was trying not to laugh.

'Ha! You're teasing me,' he laughed.

'What would you like? Eggs, ham, cheese and apple, other cereal . . .' The list continued but he'd already decided on ham, cheese and apple and a glass of orange juice.

They were making him a packed lunch to take on his trip when the backdoor opened and Granddad came in.

'I didn't know you were out,' said the boy, 'were you checking on my tree?'

'Been shopping,' replied Granddad and handed him a local supermarket bag.

Liam peered in, yelped with happiness and pulled out a baseball cap, in army green colours.

'Oh wow, thanks Granddad you're the best,' he shouted and ran to hug the old man. The boy started to cough and went red in the face.

'Do you want your puffer love?' said Gran looking worried.

Liam bent over, hands on knees and shook his head, he finally managed to squeeze out, 'I'm fine, just got a bit of apple skin stuck in my throat,' and within seconds he was bouncing out into the hallway to look in the mirror at his new cap. His grandparents could hear him talking to himself, 'hmm that's better, or maybe this way, doesn't matter anything's better than the silly hat,' and he wandered back into the kitchen wearing it back to front.

'Very nice,' said Granddad, 'but make sure you wear it the other way round if you're facing into the sun.'

'I will,' he answered and ran off upstairs to find his backpack.

After Gran had left for work, Granddad told Liam to check he'd got everything he needed. 'Lunch, drinks, puffer, I s'pose I'd better take this fold up jacket,' he decided,' and I don't think I'll need my Gameboy or torch or Torn Teddy.'

'Who or what is Torn Teddy, I thought it was girls who kept a load of junk in their bags?' said Granddad.

'He's my lucky teddy that I got from the grabbing machine last year, don't you remember. But one arm's falling off now and he's lost an eye?' answered Liam, fondly stroking the tiny teddy's head. 'I'm too big for him now, but Mum made me bring him.' That wasn't quite true, but he didn't want Granddad to think he was a baby.

'Best he doesn't go then,' answered Granddad, 'leave him here on the table and maybe Gran can fix him up.'

PART 3   LIAM

When they arrived at the Holiday Park office, Gran was behind the reception desk, talking to a tall young man and girl.

'Here's my grandson Liam,' she smiled, 'and Liam this is Peter and his girlfriend, Rosie, they'll be taking you for your adventure walk.'

'Hi,' said Liam shyly.

Peter stuck out his hand and solemnly said, 'Pleased to meet you Liam,' then gave a great big smile and said, 'are you ready for this great adventure?'

'Hi Liam, I like your hat,' added Rosie, causing the boy to grin and turn his cap the wrong way round.

While the grown ups went over some last minute details of the adventure walk, Liam wandered around the office. It hadn't changed much and still had the same display of leaflets of local places of interest. The notice board had posters up for today's walk, an archery afternoon later in the week a painting competition and all sorts of information about the Holiday Park. The biggest and brightest poster was for the end of season party in August. Liam had only been to one once, when his mum and dad had spent an extra weekend here. He hoped they could come back again this year and that he'd be allowed to join in the races and swimming, without mum flapping about him getting sick.

Chapter 26

He was brought out of his daydream by the door being flung open and a breathless voice saying, 'Have the adventure walkers gone yet, Sylvia?' Liam turned to see a plump, pretty girl with a small boy by her side.

'No, they're still here, Katie, and we're waiting for another two to turn up,' replied Gran. 'Hi Josh, do you remember seeing Liam before, he's my grandson and staying with us for a week?'

Liam and Josh just stared at each other, then Liam asked, 'How old are you?'

'Nearly nine,' said Josh, 'and I can stand on my head.'

'I'm ten,' responded Liam 'I can't stand on my head now or my hat will fall off.' He just said, because he couldn't and he didn't want the younger boy to laugh at him.

'Take it off then,' said Josh with a puzzled look on his face.

'Maybe later, have you done this walk before?' said Liam changing the subject. Before Josh could reply, a man came in holding hands with two children. They both looked the same with missing front teeth, and were wearing matching jeans and T.shirts. They had curly red hair, lots of freckles and big mischievous grins. Liam recognised them as the twins he'd seen last year they'd teased him. He was sure one had a girls name but he didn't know which.

'Here they are, William and Samantha,' said Gran and introduced them to Peter and Rosie.

'Actually I'm Wills and this is Sammy,' said one of the twins.

'Hi,' mumbled Liam.

'My brother's called Sam,' said Josh. 'He hates being called Sammy, he says it's too wussy.' Liam turned away, sniggering, he was hoping the twins wouldn't remember him and say mean things again.

But Wills ignored Josh and said, 'hey look Sammy, it's Puffer Boy.'

Before he could think of an answer, Peter jumped in with, 'come on you lot, let's get going. See that backpack over there, it's got prizes in for today's winners.'

All four children turned towards his pointing finger, Sammy tried to get away from her father to have a closer inspection, but he pulled her back and told both twins to behave, be nice and be polite, or they would be grounded. The twins just looked at each other and grinned.

Peter led the way towards the woods, while Rosie stayed at the back of the little group. When they got to the narrow path Liam found himself behind Wills. He figured this out because Wills was wearing trainers with blue laces and Sammy's laces were yellow, he hoped they wouldn't swap shoes. Wills suddenly stopped and Liam bumped into him, so Sammy purposely bumped into Liam and Josh bumped into her.

'Hey you guys, what's going on?' Rosie laughed.

'We like to see how many people get bumped, it's better if we're walking in two's, like when we go on a school trip,' Sammy answered with the same gappy grin on her face.

Being 'bumped' both back and front caused Liam to let out a gasping 'oooofff.'

'You ok puffer boy?' asked Wills

'Course I am, we do this all the time at school as well, *and* don't call me puffer boy.'

'Why do you call him that?' asked Josh.

Before the giggling twins could answer Liam shouted, 'Cos I'm like a puff adder, I can blow myself up to look big and fierce and eat twins for dinner.'

'Wow hope I don't make you cross,' said Rosie. 'Come on guys, be nice to each other, we've got a great day ahead,'

They carried on in single file and Liam heard Sammy whispering to Josh, he hoped it wasn't about him, he'd have to try and do something cool, to stop the teasing.

Chapter 27

During the walk Peter and Rosie pointed out all sorts of things, yukky looking fungus, birds' nests, trails that had been made by foxes, badgers or small deer. They also listened to different birdcalls and they even had to stop and sniff the air to see who could smell something funny. The smell had come from a fox and all the children said they did notice it, secretly they all hoped that they had actually smelt the right thing. Eventually they came to a clearing in the woods and Peter said they'd sit and have a drink, while he handed out competition work sheets for them to look at and make sure they could all read and understand the words and recognise the pictures.

'Easy,' said Wills.

'No problem,' said Sammy.

'What's this word?' asked Josh, who wasn't very good at reading yet.

'Bramble, where blackberries come from, and really prickly,' said Liam helpfully.

They all looked at their papers and Peter gave them each a pencil to write things down and a bag to put collected stuff in.

'Leave your back packs here,' he said, 'Rosie and I will look after them. Follow me so I can show you where you'll be hunting.'

The four children followed him for a while and soon they came to some red and white plastic tape that was threaded in and around trees and bushes, some of it couldn't be seen.

'If you think you're lost, just follow the tape and you'll come back to where we are now,' he smiled, 'is everyone happy with that?' All four nodded. 'Don't go the other side of the tape, but if you get really worried, shout as loud as you can, let's hear you shout.' They all did and laughed when a pigeon suddenly flew out of a nearby tree in fright. 'Right then, let's go back to Rosie, if you need anything from your bag get it now, then you can go,' said Peter. While the twins were digging about in their bags, Liam quickly got his puffer out and put it in his trouser pocket, hoping no one would notice.

'Anya's got one of those, to help her breathe,' piped up Josh. Liam's heart sank, 'who's Anya?'

'She's in my class at school, she can't run very fast.'

'Well I can breathe ok and run fast if I want to,' said Liam crossly and before anyone said anything else, he said, 'Can we go now Peter?'

'Yes, but make your way back when you hear this,' said Peter pulling a big silver whistle from his pocket and blowing hard.

Rosie sent them off in different directions and said 'No cheating, remember to follow the tape if you get lost, see you all soon.'

Chapter 28

It was cool and quiet in the woods and a bit spooky on his own, but Liam wanted to be the winner and finish first, so he started to run, looking around as he went. He collected things on the list as he saw them. Suddenly he saw the flash of something white and furry from the corner of his eye, maybe a rabbit's tail, he went after it. He was crouching and running so low, he didn't realise he'd gone under the tape. He saw it again; it was a white tail, but too big and fluffy for a rabbit. He decided to run faster and getting out of breath he reached in his pocket for his puffer. He was just about to put it in his mouth, when he tripped over a tree root, went flying through the air and fell with a thud and a grunt to the floor. His puffer shot out of his hand and disappeared into the undergrowth.

Liam lay gasping and wheezing. His heart was thudding and his first thought was, 'I need to find my puffer, I can't breathe.' Worrying like this didn't help, but Liam was too scared to calm down. He struggled to his knees, and tried to suck in deep gulps of air, but it wasn't working. Despite his panic he heard a scuffling noise and looked up to see a grey and white dog, scrabbling in the undergrowth near where he'd seen his puffer go. He knelt as still as he could and concentrated on trying to breathe deeply while he watched the dog. It eventually found something—the puffer. The dog picked it up in its mouth, then just sat and stared at Liam. The boy stretched his hand out towards the dog, he tried to say something but his voice was just a gasp.

PART 3   LIAM

All sorts of strange things went through Liam's head. He'd never complain about his mum fussing him again, Gran and Granddad would be worrying about him, he was going to die, why wouldn't the dog give him his puffer, why did the dog have one blue eye and one brown one?

Liam's gasping gradually turned to deep breathing, his heart slowed down and he knew he was fine, he was going to live. He lay down, his breathing returned to normal and he looked up at the leaves rustling in the trees, sunlight peeking through. He became aware of the dog coming over to him; it sniffed his face around his nose and mouth, then lay down by his side, leaving the puffer on the ground between its paws. Liam didn't know many dogs, thanks to his fussing Mum, so he sat up looked it in the eyes and said, 'Have you got allergies, whatever they are, if so I don't want to get them?'

The dog looked at him; Liam reached out a hand and patted it on the head. It seemed to like that so he ruffled it under the chin and felt a chain of some sort. He knew from friends with dogs, that they had to wear collars with their name and address on. He felt around the neck and found a metal disc, it was worn and he could see that there was a phone number but he couldn't read it. The other side had a very faded short name on it. Squinting and twisting the disc about to catch sunlight, Liam could just make out the word Taz.

'Hi Taz,' he said 'thanks for finding my puffer.' The dog looked at Liam cocked its head to one side, then stood up. It picked up the puffer and ran off into the trees.

Liam stood up and yelped, he'd really hurt a knee when he fell. Rolling up his trouser leg, he saw a deep, bleeding graze surrounded by a huge red mark already turning into a blue bruise. He didn't know what to do,

80

should he follow the dog? Then he heard a distant whistle and decided he'd better go back to the others, he picked up his bag of collected things and stumbled back the way he'd come. He'd try and find the dog again another day and tell Gran he'd lost his puffer, but not that he'd lost it in a dog's mouth. She might be able to get him another one from the local doctor.

Limping a lot, Liam found his way back to the tape and eventually back to the clearing.

All the others were there already going through the things they'd found.

'Hey Liam, you ok?' Rosie came over to him, looking concerned.

'Yeah, I just tripped and hurt my knee,' said Liam, 'it'll be alright.' He sat down and while Rosie treated his knee with stuff from the first aid kit, the three other children gathered round to watch.

'Whew! That's nice big scraze,' said Sammy looking impressed. Liam frowned, 'what's a scraze, you mean graze?'

'It's what my Mum says. It's not a scrape and not a graze, a bit of each,' Sammy grinned.

'Just think of the lovely scab you'll end up with to pick off,' added her brother.

'You're going to end up with a cool scar,' said Josh not to be outdone.

'Oh you horrible lot,' laughed Peter, 'seriously are you alright Liam?'

'Yes thanks, fine,' said the boy, feeling pleased with all the attention.

'I bet you cried,' said Josh.

'No way, too tough for that.' Liam answered and limped away to get his bag.

Chapter 29

The rest of the adventure walk went well. They went to the river shore and found lots of jellyfish that hadn't gone back out with the tide. They found tiny fish and sea anemones in the rock pools and kept seeing wiggly lines of sand appearing as worms dug their way into it. Liam managed to find a small crab, which he picked up and held out to Sammy, she didn't like it she thought it was like a spider. Despite his sore leg, Liam chased her and pretended to put it in her hair.

While she yelled and shook her head, her brother watched and laughed and said, 'You're ok really Puffer Boy.' Liam decided he didn't mind the nickname now at least it was said in a non-teasing way.

'If I'm Puffer Boy, I'll have to think of a name for you,' he grinned.

'What?' said Wills.

'Dunno I'll think of something.'

'Come on kids, let's find somewhere, we can sit and have lunch,' called Rosie.

'How about here?' Josh yelled, 'we can look for stuff in this rockpool at the same time.' They ran over and agreed it was an ok place, there were some large flat stones to sit on or lean against. They chatted while they ate and swapped food items, as they decided that grown ups never packed up the right stuff. All the children boasted at some point about what they'd found and seen in the woods. Sammy said she'd seen a crow in the sky being chased away by two other birds.

'How'd you know it was a crow?' her brother frowned.

'Cos it was big and black, bigger than a blackbird.'

PART 3   LIAM

'P'raps it was a rook,' Liam answered.

'Probably a crow, I've heard a lot this year and we haven't seen any rooks nests,' said Peter. 'But it might have been a kite chasing off the crow, Sammy.'

'A kite? You're nuts,' sneered Wills.

'It's a kind of bird, I've got a picture here in this book,' Rosie said fumbling in her bag. She handed the book to Wills, who started flicking through the pages. Eventually he sat back, put his thumb in his mouth and studied the 'Kite' page. Liam stared at him, he couldn't believe his luck. 'How old are you, Thumbsuck Boy?' he casually asked.

Sammy answered, 'We're going to be ten next week.'

Wills snatched his thumb from his mouth and mumbled, 'Got something stuck in my tooth.'

Josh sniggered as Liam just said, 'Yeah right.'

After lunch, Peter gave the children about ten minutes to find a list of things from the shore. He kept them all in sight and when he called them back they all broke into a run.

Sammy and Liam got back just ahead of the other two. Sammy was red in the face and panting, while Liam bent over in his usual gasping position, hands on knees and fighting for breath.

'Where's your puffer?' Rosie asked him a concerned look on her face.

'Don't need it, I'm alright.'

Wills looked on with a silly smile on his face.

Liam stood upright, 'I'm as much out of breath as Sammy, you're ok aren't you?' he nodded at the girl.

'Course I am.'

'Well have a puff to be on the safe side,' added Peter.

Liam didn't know what to do, so he said, 'Ok,' turned his back on the group, pretended to pull something out

83

of his bag and made a huge sucking noise, with his hands near his face. He wandered back to the group and looked at Wills waiting for a comment, but the boy kept quiet.

Back at the Holiday Park, they sat at a table in the picnic area and emptied out their goody bags. Rosie and Peter made a big show of checking everyone's stuff, had a quick whisper with each other and then looked at the four eager faces.

'Right,' said Peter, 'first prize, for the woods treasure finding, goes to Sammy.'

'Oh not fair, we picked the same stuff at the same time,' whined her brother.

'You shouldn't have been working together.' Rosie tried to put on a stern face

Peter took no notice. 'First prize for being first one back from the woods treasure hunt, goes to,' he paused and looked at Josh, 'Wills,' he said. Wills whooped and Josh looked away, his lip trembling.

Rosie joined in then, 'First prize for the beach treasure hunt, goes to Josh.' He then gave a great big smile and said, 'Thank you.' 'And first prize for first back from the beach treasure hunt goes to . . .' 'LIAM,' they all shouted, clapped and cheered. Peter and Rosie gave each child a gold coloured medal on a red and blue ribbon. They proudly hung them around their necks and Rosie got them lined up along one bench seat to have their photo' taken.

When Rosie said, 'Say cheese,' Liam, who was now able to joke with his new mate, Wills, said, 'You'd better not, we might all fall in the gap in your mouth.'

Everyone fell about laughing, Wills and Sammy, made even bigger grins to show the missing teeth gaps, Josh bent over holding his sides, even Peter and Rosie joined in, until she said 'keep still you lot or I can't get a picture.'

Chapter 30

Later, back at his grandparents' house, Liam sat on the kitchen worktop, while Gran bathed his sore knee with warm salty water. He hadn't stopped chattering about the great day he'd had, but he didn't mention his puffer. Once when he paused for breath, Gran said, 'Did you need your puffer?'

'No, Gran I keep telling you I'm fine,' he replied loudly, then seeing her face take on a cross look, he quickly added, 'really, don't worry.'

She smiled and said, 'Ok, but don't try to be tough and not use it, if you run out of breath.'

Liam suddenly had a picture in his head of the dog with one brown and one blue eye, holding the puffer in its mouth and wondered whether to tell Gran he'd lost it. He decided to wait till later, when they weren't talking about it anymore. With his knee cleaned up he slid down from the worktop and went to find Granddad in the garden, while Gran got dinner ready.

'Do the people next door, still have a dog?' he casually asked the old man.

'Yes, I don't see it much now, it's getting old, like me,' smiled Granddad.

'I've forgotten its name,' said Liam,' I wish I could have a dog, but Mum would worry about germs.'

This started to chat about dogs, then cats and other pets and each time Liam added, 'I wish I could have . . .'

Eventually Granddad said he'd take him along to the animal shelter to meet Jackie and her rescued animals again, one day in the week, which Liam was waiting for. He loved it there.

After dinner, the boy made a big show of unpacking his backpack, then pretending to be surprised he said, 'I can't find my puffer.'

Gran made him check his trouser pockets, while Granddad went through the backpack again.

'I must've dropped it when I tripped over, I'd better go and look,' said Liam, wanting to go and find Taz with the strange eyes.

'Not now, it's getting late,' said Gran. 'We'll go and look in the morning.'

Liam didn't want anyone to go with him, so he told a little white lie. 'Actually I must've left it at the picnic table when we unpacked our treasure,' he said. 'I can have a look in the morning while you go to the office, Gran.'

'Alright love,' she said, 'but come to the office first in case someone has found it and handed it in.'

While he was lying in bed later, Liam thought about the day he'd had. He hoped to meet up with the other kids again, but it wouldn't be until the end of season party. Josh was lucky, he came here every weekend, but Wills and Sammy had only been for a week, they were going home tomorrow. Maybe I'll meet Taz again thought Liam and made all sorts of plans in his head, to try and get away on his own sometimes. Luckily his grandparents weren't as strict as his mum they often let him go out alone as long as he didn't go too far. All this thinking made Liam really tired and soon he fell into a deep sleep.

Chapter 31

'Good morning, you're an early bird today,' Granddad greeted him in the kitchen.

'I like to get up early when I'm here, there's so much good stuff to do, are we going to Jackie's?' he answered.

'Maybe after lunch, Gran's working till three today,' said Granddad.

'Great I'm just going to go and look for my puffer,' said the boy heading to the back door.

'After breakfast young man, slow down,' said Gran, who had just come into the room, then she said, 'I don't have to be in until eleven, can it wait till then?'

'Noooooo, someone might find it and take it,' replied Liam impatiently, then he came out with one of his ideas. 'The twins are going home today, if I see them can I play for a while, before they leave?'

'That should be ok, they usually go about midday, but don't get in their way,' said Gran. Secretly she was thinking that the twins parents usually told them to keep out of the way while they packed up to go home, so the children could all get together at the play park.

Great, thought Liam and hoped he wouldn't see the twins too soon, 'cos he wanted to see Taz first.

As soon as he'd finished breakfast, he grabbed his hat, asked Gran for a drink and snack to take with him and rushed off, shouting, 'I'll be back before twelve, byee.'

'He's in a hurry, it's good to see him so relaxed and happy,' said his Gran to her husband, 'Sue fusses over him far too much.'

The old man just grunted something about 'women' and went out to the garden.

Liam ran fast, hoping to not see anyone he knew and have to stop and talk, he ran past the swimming pool, the picnic area and finally reached the path into the woods. He had a good memory and recognised a lot of the things that Peter had pointed out the day before. It wasn't long before he came to the clearing and he sat down to catch his breath. He didn't want to rest, but he thought it might be an idea, 'just in case.' As he opened up his backpack he heard a stick or something crack, in the bushes behind him, he sat very still holding his breath and straining to hear for any other strange noises. Slowly he turned his head and there was Taz, just standing and looking at him.

Liam patted the ground beside him and said, 'Here boy, come on.' The dog wandered over and sniffed at Liam, his outstretched hand, his head and then around the boy's mouth and nose.

'Hey, what's all that for,' laughed Liam, but Taz just stared at him, put his head on one side and sat on his hind legs. The two stared at each other Liam stroked the dog's face and peered really hard into his strange eyes. His fur was a dark and light grey and he had long silky white hair over his chest. His tail was all three colours too, with a tiny little bit of brown near the tip.

'I wonder what sort of dog you are, you look like my friend's collie dog, but he's black and white. Doesn't matter I think you're nice as you are,' murmured Liam. Then he remembered his reason for trying to find the dog and said, 'What've you done with my puffer?'

Taz carried on staring at Liam then he pushed his nose into the boy's hand and licked it, then sniffed around the open backpack.

'Ha!' said Liam 'Are you after my snack?' and so saying he pulled a packet of cheesy biscuits from his bag and teased the patient dog, pretending to open them under his nose. Taz raised a paw and Liam realised he wanted to shake hands, he'd obviously been taught this trick to get a treat.

'Hang on then,' said Liam and gently shook Taz's paw, then the two settled down and shared the packet of biscuits. 'All gone,' said the boy, putting the empty packet into his bag, 'come on show me where my puffer is.'

Taz jumped up and started to run, with Liam close behind. Watching the dog so closely Liam didn't really notice where they were going, until suddenly they came out of the woods, went past a little cottage and out onto a big field.

Liam shouted, 'Stop Taz, where are we, I need to catch my breath?' He looked around and suddenly realised they were on the field opposite the lane where his grandparents lived. At the bottom of the field was the duck pond, it looked as though the dog was headed there.

Oh gosh, thought Liam, what am I going to say if Gran or Granddad see me? Thankfully the grass and weeds were quite high and hopefully he wouldn't be seen very easily if he stooped as he ran. Luckily their house was set back a bit from the road so they couldn't see him anyway, unless they were at the end of the driveway.

Finally he reached the pond and threw himself down under the hanging branches of a willow tree. Taz was scrabbling about near the water's edge and looked up, he had the puffer in his mouth.

'Good boy, bring it here,' said Liam, panting for breath, but despite words like, 'leave,' 'give,' 'drop,' the dog just sat and stared, then he turned and jumped into the pond, puffer in his mouth and swam into a huge bunch of bulrushes. Several moorhens came swimming out and chattering in distress, but Taz ignored them. Liam looked on in surprise as the dog swam back to shore with an empty mouth.

'What have you done, you silly dog?' yelled the boy crossly. Taz slowly climbed out of the water, again he nuzzled Liam's face, then shook himself so hard that drops of pond water showered over the cross little boy. At that Liam broke into a smile, then laughed and said, 'Know what Taz, I don't think I need it. I need to go now, I'll tell Gran I couldn't find it,' and off he ran towards home. He turned and saw Taz running in the opposite direction towards the cottage, they'd passed before.

Chapter 32

Liam ran past his grandparents' house and carried on into the Holiday Park. He passed a car leaving the site, which turned out to be the twins and their parents.

'See ya in August Puffer Boy,' shouted Wills, winding down a window. Liam stopped and watched the car, he waved at the two grinning faces, looking out of the back window.

I won't have to tell a lie now, he thought. I have seen the twins. He reached the reception office and saw Gran talking to another customer, glancing at the clock, he saw it was nearly midday and told himself he'd timed it just right.

'Hi love any luck with the puffer?' Gran asked

'No, it wasn't at the picnic area, did anyone hand it in here?' he asked knowing quite well that no one had.

'No, not yet. To be on the safe side we'll make an appointment at the local doctors' surgery and get you another.'

'Ok, when will you be back Gran?'

'Just after 3 o clock, run on home, Granddad knows what's for lunch, I'll see you later.' Liam went, thankful that Gran hadn't asked him where he'd been.

After lunch in the garden, Liam and his granddad went off in the car to visit the animal rescue place. The lady who ran it was called Jackie and she introduced Liam to several rabbits, a ferret, some hedgehogs and a few cats. She told him the story of the little tabby cat called Tam, who'd been rescued by a boy called Jack.

'I remember that,' said Granddad, 'he made a lovely poster, Gran put it up in reception, but no one claimed the kitten.'

'Well he's very happy now,' smiled Jackie. Hearing about Tam, reminded Liam about Taz and he wondered if he'd get the chance to see him again and what excuses he could make to get away on his own.

Chapter 33

The next morning Gran took Liam along to the local Doctors' surgery.

'Are you going to tell Mum, I lost my puffer,' Liam asked, 'last time I lost it, she got really cross.'

'Well if she sees you've got another one, she might not be.'

Doctor Vincent had a kind, smiley face and when he heard that Liam had lost his puffer, he said he couldn't let him have a new one, unless he checked the boy over first. He looked in his mouth, up his nose and in his ears with little things like very bright torches. He listened to Liam's chest and back with a thing called a stethoscope which was a long rubber tube with ear plugs on one end and a flat plastic thing on the other. He made the boy breathe really deeply and blow out as much as he could, then he asked him to run very fast on the spot.

After that, Liam was red in the face and breathing and gasping really heavily; he took up his usual position of bending over with hands on knees. Gran looked concerned but Dr. Vincent just smiled and said, 'Stand up straight and breathe deeply. Well-done Liam, that's all, put your T-shirt back on.' He then asked Gran, how long Liam had been using a puffer and all sorts of other questions. He asked Liam if he played football or went swimming and seemed surprised when the boy said, 'Mum doesn't like me to, in case I get a bad breathing attack.'

'All Mum's worry about their children, mine still worries about me,' laughed the doctor. Then he added, 'I

93

can find no sign of any breathing problem whatsoever, so I'm not going to give you another puffer. The reason you get out of breath so quickly is because you're not working your heart and your lungs enough. To make that happen you have to get fitter by lots of breathing hard to get more oxygen in. You need to be more sporty, Liam, run more, swim more.' Dr. Vincent explained this very carefully so the boy would understand.

Gran smiled and smiled and Liam shouted, 'Wow great, come on Gran let's go swimming.'

That afternoon, Liam and his grandfather went to the pool while Gran had to work. He had a great time and Granddad taught him how to float how to tread water and all sorts of water stuff. Liam wanted to be able to swim fast, so he could enter the races in August and Granddad gave him some ideas of how to swim better.

'Hey Granddad can you teach me to dive?' Liam asked when he saw some other children jumping in.

'No it's not really deep enough, look see that sign,' he pointed, 'No Diving.'

'Oh,' grumbled the boy, but soon cheered up when his grandfather allowed him to join in with the jumping.

'I've had enough Liam,' said Granddad, 'do you want to stay in, while I sit and watch?'

'Yes please, I'm going to ask those other kids if they want to have a jumping competition.'

The old man looked at the other children, there was one boy there that he'd seen before and thought he was a bit of a bully.

'Just be careful,' he said. Liam had also recognised the boy from last year and remembered his Mum telling Gran that she didn't want Liam anywhere near him. He was used to being teased and picked on and, having recently made friends with Wills, he had an idea of how to talk to the 'bully.' He went over where the boy was standing on the side, ready to jump.

'Hi,' Liam said, 'you're good at this can you show me how to do it?'

Pleased to show off the boy, swung his arms and threw himself off the side, making a huge splash. 'S' easy, just like that,' he grinned. Liam had a go and made it look as though he was scared.

The bully boy laughed climbed out and did it again, 'Don't think about it, just go,' he said.

After a few more times, Liam asked the boy what his name was. 'Max,' was the answer, 'what's yours?'

'Liam,' then he added, 'let's see who can jump the furthest away from the end.'

Chapter 34

Walking back to the house later, Liam said, 'Max is alright,' Granddad, 'I let him win most of the time, so he won't pick on me.'

'I think Max is quite shy really, which is why he shows off and pretends to be tough,' said Granddad, secretly pleased that Liam had made a friend. 'You must be starving, young man, let's go have a piece of Gran's home-made chocolate cake and a drink.'

'I thought she was saving that for tea at the weekend, when mum and Dad come for me?'

Granddad winked, 'She always makes two.'

'What shall we do after?' asked Liam.

'I want to sit out in the garden and read my paper, what do you want to do?'

'Can I go down to the pond and see if the ducks and moorhens are about and take some bread for them?' Liam was hoping to meet up with Taz.

'I don't want to walk all the way over there, you've tired me out today Liam, we'll go tomorrow,' said Granddad.

'Oh please, you don't have to come, I'm nearly eleven, I'll be really careful and keep off the road, you'll still be able to see me,' pleaded the boy.

'We'll see, let's have our cake first.'

It was really nice and peaceful in the garden and Liam could see Granddad was getting very dozey behind his newspaper. His head kept drooping, then he'd snort and sit up straight and rustle the paper a lot.

'I'm off to the pond now Granddad,' said Liam, fingers crossed.

'Hmm. What? Ok just be careful, don't be long,' but Liam had already disappeared up the driveway, where he collected the bag of bread he'd left there while Granddad was getting their cake and drinks.

He ran all the way and kept looking towards the cottage where he thought the dog lived and then, just as he reached the water's edge, Taz came bounding over. The two greeted each other in a tangle of legs and paws, wet licks and heavy pats on the head. Liam threw himself down on the grass and patted the ground beside him. Taz came and sat and looked at the interesting rustling bag in Liam's hand. 'It's bread for the birds,' Liam said to the dog, 'you're not a bird.' Taz held up his paw, so Liam gave in and offered a crust. He chattered away, told the dog about his trip to the doctor's and to the swimming pool, pausing now and again to ruffle the dog's soft, furry head or throw bread to the ducks. As the last crust hit the water, Taz jumped in swam off to the bulrushes again and returned with Liam's puffer in his mouth.

Liam laughed, 'I don't need it now, silly, but thanks anyway.' Then he thought, 'Where shall I tell Gran I found it?' As he was thinking what to say, Taz kept pushing his nose towards the pocket of the boy's shorts. Eventually Liam realised what the dog was telling him, 'My pocket! But not the jeans I was wearing. I'll say it was in my jacket. Good thinking Taz.'

The two friends sat there a while longer, then Liam heard his grandfather shouting for him.

He jumped up, 'Ssee you soon boy,' and off he ran. 'I wasn't too long was I Granddad?' he asked when he got back.

'No you're ok. What's that in your pocket?'

'Just the bag the bread was in, I'll go throw it away,' he answered, 'then I'd better wash my hands.' He made a big show of throwing the rubbish in the bin, then ran indoors and upstairs to hide his puffer and wash his hands.

Chapter 35

The rest of the week went by much too fast. Liam swam at the pool again, with Max and one day it was a bit cloudy so Liam asked Granddad if they could go to the camp play area and kick a football about. Again other children joined in and Liam really enjoyed running about and getting red in the face. He decided he'd be really fit and ready for the end of season races, he was determined to make his parents come here for that weekend.

Gran didn't have to work at all on Friday, so the three of them went for an open top bus ride, to the local town. When it started to spit with rain, Liam got his waterproof jacket from his backpack and pretended to be really surprised when he pulled his puffer from the pocket.

'I thought you'd checked your pockets,' said Gran laughing.

'I did, but only my jeans, Granddad checked the backpack,' he grinned.

'Your jacket was rolled up, I didn't think of that. Doesn't matter now anyway,' he gave the boy a quick hug.

'I wonder what Mum and Dad'll say,' said Liam.

'They'll take one look at this tanned, happy face and say, Where's our boy, what have you done with him, who's this stranger?' Gran made a worried looking face while closing her eyes and putting one hand over her heart. Liam and Granddad roared with laughter.

'Poor Sue, we shouldn't laugh at her, she has been really worried over you in the past,' Gran said

'Well now she can relax and hopefully join in all the fun you're going to have' Granddad poked Liam in the ribs making him squeal and laugh again.

He was very quiet after tea and his grandmother knew exactly what was the matter.

'Cheer up love, now you're really better I'm sure your mum and dad will bring you back again at the end of August.'

'I hope so Gran, but there is something I'd like to do now all by myself, while it's still light. Can I go visit the pond and say goodbye to the dog, er ducks?'

'Yes dear, straight there and straight back,' she smiled and watched him run off down the driveway. Luckily no one had noticed his mistake.

Liam was up early on Saturday, he wanted to make the most of his last day here. He'd been tearful when he'd said 'goodbye' to Taz the day before, and now he had an idea to help keep the dog close in his heart. After breakfast he went to his room to pack his things and there sitting in the middle of his bed was 'Torn Ted,' only now he had a little black patch sewn over one eye and a fabulous wooden peg leg. Liam laughed, 'Granddad remembered, he's now 'Tough Ted.' Liam had something else he wanted to do so he was upstairs for ages. He packed his stuff and kept picking Tough Ted up and having pirate like talks with him. Granddad called him down for a mid morning snack and asked him what he'd been up to. 'Nothing really, just thinking and packing and playing pirates, thanks for helping Torn Ted Gran and Granddad,' said Liam. 'Can I go and say goodbye to Max and your office friends Gran?'

'Why don't you wait and see if your parents are going to bring you back in August for the End of Season Party, then you can tell them the news.'

'Good idea, let's go check my oak tree instead.'

As the boy and his granddad were looking at the tree, which had finally been planted on the edge of the driveway, his parent's car pulled up. Waving hard, Liam dashed back down the drive and shouted to Gran through the kitchen window. 'They're here, Mum and Dad are here.' He raced back again, just as his mother stepped from the car. He threw himself at her, hugging her around her waist. 'Mum, Mum, guess what I don't need a puffer anymore.' He released her, before she could answer and running round the other side of the car, he jumped up and hung on his dad's neck, just as he was stooping to climb out.

'Wow Liam, have you grown, have they been feeding you bricks?' Dad grabbed his son and swung him round, before setting him on his feet.

Chapter 36

They had lunch in the garden and Liam let his grandparents do all the explaining about the puffer. His mother still looked concerned and said she'd still take him to their regular doctor to make sure. Liam thought his heart would burst with happiness when his parents agreed they would all come back for the long party weekend. The only shadow was that he couldn't go and tell Taz, he didn't think they'd let him go to the pond again.

'Is it ok if I go and say goodbye to Max and the others now, Gran?'

'On your own?' said Mum sounding surprised.

'He's fine Sue, a very good boy, you've got there. 'Yes dear off you go,' answered Gran.

He didn't need telling twice. He ran to the pool and told Max the good news, then went over to the office. Jean was there talking to Josh and his dad. 'Hi Josh, I've got to go home today, but I'll be back for the last weekend party,' he said.

'We always come to that too,' said Josh, 'see you then Liam.'

'You off now Liam?' Jean asked him,

'Yes but I'm coming back, so I've got to give you this,' smiled Liam, handing over a mysterious piece of paper, 'see you later Jean, and thanks.'

'I haven't done anything to be thanked for,' thought Jean as she watched the boy go running off back towards his grandparent's house.

PART 4
MOLLY

Chapter 37

'And last but not least, our final prize for continued effort goes to . . .' Mr. Miller, the headteacher made a dramatic pause, causing many of the children to hold their breath. 'Molly Newton,' he said, smiling at everyone.

A horrible silence, followed by a series of groans and 'her again' comments, filled the assembly hall. It didn't last long, because Mr. Miller started clapping enthusiastically, the other teachers and finally the students joined in. However there were no loud cheers or whistles, which had followed some of the other prizewinners.

Molly slowly got to her feet she hated this, the whole school watching her. In her mind prize for continued effort meant she hadn't improved and once again was bottom of the class. Head hanging forward so her frizzy hair hid her face, she made her way up on to the stage to receive her prize envelope—probably another book token—and to shake hands with Mr. Miller. Standing in front of him, with her back to the rest of the hall, he took her hand and said, 'Well done Molly, you've worked very hard. Come on stand up straight, be proud of yourself.' She gave him a weak smile, her brown eyes shining with tears behind her thick framed, ugly glasses.

'Thank you sir,' she muttered and turned to make her way back to her seat.

As she squeezed past other students in the same row, to get to her chair she heard Lily say, 'Nerdy Newton wins again, what a surprise.'

Sally who was sitting next to Lily replied, 'not so *nerdy* Newton, this is like the 'losers' prize.' Both girls giggled.

Pretending not to hear, Molly sat down beside Beth, who said, 'Take no notice of them Moll, aren't you going to open it?' She pointed at the envelope in Molly's hand.

'It's just another book token probably,'

'*Another* book token, ha! I'd be happy to have just one.'

'You like reading I don't,' snapped Molly and then felt bad because Beth had tried to be friendly.

Chapter 38

It was the last day of the summer term, six long weeks of holidays stretched before her. When she returned in September she'd be in the senior school and her parents would expect more from her.

Walking home alone later, Molly was dreading what her father would say about the prize. He always expected the best from his children and this would be the third time she'd received an *effort* prize. Her older brother was home from University, he had a holiday job locally and her sister was away in Egypt, working at an archaeological dig. Molly thought of herself as the family dunce. Dad was a meteorologist and was often seen on national television giving the weather forecast and her mum was a doctor of philosophy, whatever that was, at a college.

Mum's car was in the driveway when she got home, oh well, here goes, she thought, going in through the back door.

'Hi Mum.'

'Molly dear, how did prize giving go, I'm sorry I couldn't make it,' her mother replied.

'You didn't miss much, just the usual.'

'Well what did you get?' said Mum.

'How do you know if I got anything?' Molly sounded cross.

'You should, you're a Newton and you've won before.' Mum turned away to read whatever it was she was holding in her hand.

'Yeah another book token I guess,' said Molly, 'I'm going to get changed, see you.' As she left the room, her mother gave a small sigh and wondered why her youngest child was always so miserable.

Molly was a student at a very expensive private school, for 'gifted' girls. She'd just scraped through the entrance exam to get there, but she wasn't at all happy. She didn't think of herself as clever as the other girls and being shy she didn't make friends very easily. She didn't think so, but she was very kind-hearted. If she came across anyone or any creature, needing help, she did. Though where wasps were concerned, she just opened a window or door and used a rolled up paper or something to help them out. She had often looked after younger girls at school if they were in tears and she'd even helped her next door neighbour, who looked about 120 years old to clean out a disgusting drain, which had been blocked with leaves and an old dishcloth. Ugh!

'I'm not gifted, except in being stupid,' she often told herself as she struggled with homework. Sometimes she asked her parents for help, but they were stricter than her teachers *and* they were allowed to nag at her, which made her get all flustered and do things wrong.

Upstairs in her room, Molly wondered what awful project her dad would find for her to do this summer. Last year, while they were away on holiday, for goodness sake, he'd sent her off to discover what happened to different things after heavy rain.

'They get wet and sometimes soggy,' was what she wanted to say, but didn't. She'd still managed to write about six pages of stuff, including pictures she'd drawn and a collection of plastic bags containing small bits of wood, cloth, biscuit and stone as examples. Dad had frowned at this collection but didn't say anything. This year they weren't going away until the last week of the school holidays. Her dad had been asked to do a week of presenting the weather on TV, somewhere Molly had never heard of.

Chapter 39

The weeks passed and eventually Molly and her parents arrived at their holiday place. It was a caravan park near a small village in Suffolk. Looking out of the car window while Dad and Mum went to fetch a key and information from the reception office, she saw other holidaymakers wandering about. None of the children seemed to be her age, not that it mattered, as they probably wouldn't want to hang out with her anyway. She turned and looked back the way they'd come, through a spooky looking wood and suddenly she saw something run across the track and disappear into the trees.

I wonder what that was, she thought, it was too small to be a deer, maybe a wolf! Ha! There aren't any wolves in Suffolk, must've been a dog or large cat. Molly was used to talking to herself, she was usually the only one who listened.

'Here we are, take this Molly,' said Mum as she came back to the car and handed over a bunch of leaflets.

'What's this lot?'

'Just some information about this holiday park and some other leaflets about local places of interest.'

'Will we be going to any of them?' asked Molly, knowing that they probably wouldn't go anywhere unless it was a museum, library or some other old building.

'I'll be going to the television and radio studios most days,' answered Dad, 'I thought it would be nicer for you and Mum to stay here, rather than a hotel in town; anyway it fits the project I think you'll enjoy doing.'

PART 4   MOLLY

Molly groaned, she thought Dad had forgotten about wretched projects. She'd already *had* to spend an hour a day of her holiday so far, doing school work to try and improve the things that said 'needs to try harder' or 'good effort' on her school report.

They found their caravan and were unpacking the car, when a man and woman with a young boy and a girl, passed by to the caravan next door. Her parents and the other two adults said 'Hello' to each other, the girl just smiled and the boy took no notice of them. Molly disappeared behind her curtain of hair and dashed into the caravan.

'Try to be more friendly dear, a 'hello' to your neighbours won't hurt you,' said her mum, as she turned away and went back out to the car, leaving Molly looking out of a window.

The other family had gone and then a bigger boy came cycling up, skidded to a stop outside and also went in next door. Molly hoped she wouldn't bump into them too often. The quick look she'd had of the girl reminded her of Beth, from school. Long brown hair, pretty face and wearing a fashion top and shorts.

Molly was in her old jeans and a plain T-shirt. Braces on her front teeth, thick, framed glasses on her freckled nose and frizzy hair.

Chapter 40

'Ok, let's go and explore this park,' said Dad later, when they'd unpacked.

Molly didn't want to go it would end up being a lecture on whatever her parents saw that they thought she needed to know about. However in her father's words, 'No is not an option,' so out they went. Just about every person they passed, Mum smiled and nodded and Dad called out, 'Hi there.' Molly kept her head down, hands in jeans pockets and scuffed along between them.

When they came to the swimming pool, Mum said, 'Look Molly, there are the next door children, why don't you go and say hello?'

'We're exploring Mum, I've got all week to do that,' she muttered in reply and hurried on towards a picnic area, which was just a few wooden tables and bench sets with litter bins by each table. There were some small children playing with plastic toys at one, thankfully they took no notice of her.

Beyond this area was a path leading into the woods with a sign that said, To the Shore.

'That's good,' said Dad from behind, making her jump, remember this pathway Molly, you'll need to use it, for your project.'

'What's it about, this time?' sighed the girl.

'Well I thought you'd be able to help me out, you're going to find out what the weather is doing and what changes you've found around you, to make that happen'.

Molly's heart dropped, 'that's not helping you Dad, you already know this stuff,' said his daughter.

'It's about time you learned something about weather, you'll be taking Geography next year and I thought you might find it more interesting, as it's my work.'

'Can't I just watch a leaf grow?' mumbled Molly with one of her rare attempts at answering back.

'Don't be silly dear, you're old enough to know better now,' said Dad and patted her on the shoulder, 'come on let's find Mum, then we'll go food shopping.' He turned to walk back while she stood for a moment looking into the woods. A rustling sound in some undergrowth caught her attention, then suddenly a grey and white dog bounded out onto the path. Sensing her, the dog stopped, turned its head and stared at the girl. She gasped and stared back into its brown eyes. No wait a minute, only one was brown, the other was blue. She was about to call out to her dad, when the dog, shook its furry head and ran off into the greenery on the other side of the path.

'Come on Molly, what's keeping you?' her father called.

'Nothing. Ok,' she replied and hurried to catch up with him.

Chapter 41

When they'd finished their evening meal, Molly went to switch on the TV but her dad said, 'Not now Moll, I've got something much more interesting for you to look at, come here.'

She wandered over to the table where Dad was arranging loads of rolled up paperwork. Oh great she thought, here's my project. She slouched down onto one of the chairs and waited while Dad unrolled one of the papers.

'It's a map of this area,' he said, 'I've drawn it so it's easier for you to understand. Here,' he pointed, 'this is the holiday park.'

Molly looked, 'What's that?' she asked running her finger down a brown wiggly line, 'a giant worm, going through the woods.'

'Silly, that's the path we saw, which leads to the shore,' answered her dad and gave her a sharp look as he realised she was just messing about. 'Look dear, if you want to get better results at school, you must pay more attention and this kind of thing will help you.'

'Yes dad, sorry dad,' she said and tried to look interested.

During the next half-hour Dad told her what he wanted her to do. She had to go to the shore every morning at the same time and make a note of where the tide line was.

'Find something on the ground that's always in the same place to use as a marker, maybe a rock or a tree.' He said. 'You can also draw pictures of clouds, if there are any and watch to see which way the wind's blowing them.

'S'pose there's no clouds?' she asked.

'There are some trees close by and there's a flag near the boats for hire. You should be able to watch the movements made by the wind.'

Dad knew everything, she couldn't make things up, she thought. Still if she worked quickly each day, she'd have the rest of the time to do something else. Hopefully Mum wouldn't drag her to every museum and art gallery in the area. She had seen one of the leaflets from the holiday office, was advertising a local animal shelter, and one-day this week there was an arts and crafts activity for the youngsters, somewhere near the park. Molly's eleventh birthday was at the end of the week, she hoped no one would make a big deal out of it because it would fall at the same time as the big end of season party she'd heard her parents talk about.

Later after saying goodnight to her parents she went to her room and lay half-asleep, thinking about the project. Suddenly, for no reason the picture of a brown and blue eyed dog flashed through her mind.

Chapter 42

'Hi Mum, what's for breakfast?' Molly shouted, poking her head out of her bedroom doorway.

'Cereal, toast with or without dippy eggs, don't shout at me, I'm only a few feet away,' smiled Mum.

'Thanks,' Molly sat down and helped herself to cereal.

'I really can't understand why you don't put milk on it.'

'Milk spoils the taste of cereal and cereal spoils the taste of milk, 'that's why I don't have it very often and then I don't have to keep answering this question.'

'Don't be cheeky, young lady. Dad's left already, do you know what you're doing this morning, and do you want me to come with you?'

'I'll be ok Mum, I've decided to go to the shore about eleven o'clock each day, then be back for lunch. So can I take a mid morning snack with me please?'

'Yes of course, we bought stuff yesterday, for that reason.' 'What are you going to do mum?'

'Not sure' it looks as though it might rain, so I might just go over to the office and ask if I can borrow some books, from their book swap table. If the weather turns out ok we can go out together later.'

'Ok, but not a museum please.'

'We'll see, come on help clear up and pack a snack.'

Making her way towards the shore footpath, Molly tripped on a paving stone near the picnic benches. She didn't fall down, but her rolled up map went flying along with her bag containing sketch pad and pencil tin. Of course the tin fell out and burst open and of course the girl from next door and her older brother were sat at a table with some others.

'Have you come to join us?' said a boy.

'Have you come to draw us?' laughed another.

Poor Molly felt her cheeks burning as she got down on her hands and knees and scrabbled about to pick up her stuff. Why oh why did it happen right here, why had she kept all those stupid bits of pencil that she never used any more? There seemed to be hundreds of them.

'Here I'll help,' said the girl kindly, holding the tin and putting bits back in it. 'I'm Katie; I think we're next door to you at the moment.'

'Yes, thanks, I'm Molly,' she answered and was about to rush off again, when Katie pulled a hair band from her pocket, gave it to Molly.

'Take this, it's only and old one, it'll help keep the lid on.' Molly looked at her and thought how nice the girl was.

Then she mumbled, 'Thanks again,' and dashed off.

It was quite windy down on the shore and Molly looked around wondering where to start. Luckily there were no other young people about to ask what she was doing and call her nerdy. She walked towards the boat hire place and saw the flag that Dad had mentioned. It was being blown towards the direction she'd come from. The tide was out and Molly decided she'd use the end of the jetty as the marker for how far the tide came in. She climbed up the wooden ladder onto it and walked the short distance to the end, it was quite a long drop to the mud underneath. Molly shivered, the water would be quite deep if it came up to where she was standing, she wouldn't want to fall in, and she wasn't a very good swimmer.

There were a lot of small boats, dinghies, tied up and resting on the mud, some others were placed upside down and leaning against the side of the hut and some propped up on end against the river bank. She saw a poster on the door of the hut, showing when high and low tides were, boats were only hired out just before the water was at its highest. That explained why no one was around.

Molly looked up at the sky and the layers of huge, thick, dark clouds streaming across towards the land. Further out, the sky was nearly black and the wind had grown stronger. Having learned lots from her dad, she knew it was about to pour with rain. She tried the handle of the hire hut, but the door was locked, she was going to get soaked, there was no way she'd get back to the caravan before the downpour. Just then slow, fat drops of water started to fall and it wouldn't be long before they got faster. Molly grabbed her stuff and squeezed into a gap behind one of the boats leaning against the bank. It was dark, cool and damp here and she started worrying about slimy slugs and snails so she got out again as fast as she could. The rain was coming down harder now, and then she noticed one of the boats on the mud had a canvas cover over it.

'That'll do,' she shouted to herself and ran across, lifted one corner of the cover and scrambled in.

Even as quick as she was, she still managed to get quite wet. The bottom of the boat was a bit damp, but at least no water was getting in over her head. It was dark in here too, but there were little bits of daylight around the edges of the cover, where it was stretched up over the stuff in the little boat. Molly half sat and half lay on the floor, her back resting against a rolled up canvas bundle, which she thought was probably a sail. She fumbled in her bag for a snack, a cereal bar—no milk with this—and a packet of mini chocolate biscuits. While she ate the chewy bar she daydreamed about pirates and rough seas. The rain beat down hard above her head, but as she was snug and beginning to warm up, she dozed off to sleep.

Chapter 43

Pins and needles in her arm brought Molly awake. It was quiet no sound of rain. She sat up rubbed her arm and peered out from her shelter and gasped in horror. Her boat was floating; it didn't appear to be tied to anything. The tide had come in and she was a long way from the shore, she could just see the jetty platform, but the steps to it were completely underwater. She started crying; she was scared and thought she was going to die.

'Oh please let me be ok, please let me be ok,' she whispered to herself. 'I'll do projects with Dad for the rest of my life, please, please.'

Suddenly she heard something, she held her breath and listened, and there it was again. Turning towards the riverbank, Molly saw a streak of grey and white through her misted up glasses. She quickly took them off, wiped them clean and put them on again. She saw a dog and it was looking towards the water and barking. She waved to it and shouted, 'Hey.'

The dog jumped into the water and started swimming towards the boat. Molly watched, while patting the side of the boat and saying, 'Come on dog, come on.' All she could see was the dog's head slicing through the water towards her, she couldn't believe it, again, she was looking into two strange eyes, one brown and one blue.

The dog swam around to the front of the boat and picked up a rope trailing in the water, holding it firmly in strong jaws, it made its way back towards the shore. Feeling a bit braver now she had help, Molly knelt at the front of the boat and paddled with her hands.

It wasn't long before the dog stumbled and Molly realised it was now walking.

'Thank you, thank you, good dog,' she said and climbed out of the boat and into the water which came up to her knees. She didn't care about wet jeans and trainers, as she was so relieved to be back on land. Taking the rope from the dog's mouth, she pulled the boat in closer to the shore and tied it to a heavy chain, which she saw had a few others tied to it. Turning back towards her rescuer, she got on her knees and threw her arms around its neck. It pulled away and shook so hard that Molly got sprayed with water. She laughed and held out a hand.

'Are you a boy or girl?' she said and as it came to sniff her fingers, she felt around the wet furry neck for a collar. She found a chain with a very worn nametag hanging from it. Squinting through dog-splashed glasses, Molly read what was engraved there.

'Well thank you very much Taz,' she said, 'what can I give you for a reward?'

Taz turned back towards the boat he reached his head over the side of it and returned with the mini chocolate biscuits in his mouth. Luckily Molly had dozed off before she'd had time to eat them in the boat

'Clever boy,' she said, 'how did you know, did you smell them?'

The storm was over and the two sat and shared the biscuits. Well, she had one and Taz had the rest. She talked and he listened.

'Everyone wants me to be clever, like the rest of my family, but I don't care now, I'll still try my best, but at least I'm alive.' Then she thought how daft that sounded, she wouldn't have died, there were oars in the boat. She'd just been so scared, she hadn't thought of them at the time. Taz nuzzled her hand and licked her chin. Molly gave him a hug and stood up, 'are you coming back with me Taz. You must live around here I've seen you before?'

He also stood up and wagged his tail.

'Hang on,' she said 'I'll just get the rest of my stuff from the boat.' She turned away to collect her things and was pulling the canvas cover back over the boat, when she heard a shout from the top of the bank.

'Molly, where are you?'

It was her mum. Grabbing everything she hurried towards her mother.

'There you are, I was worried, about you, you've been gone so long and then there was that awful rainstorm, are you alright?'

'I'm fine Mum, the hut's closed so I sheltered in a boat and it . . .' she stopped, she didn't want to worry her mother.

'It what,'

'It was fun,' said the girl, looking around.

'Have you got everything, what are you looking for?' said Mum. 'Yes, nothing, oh just that empty rubbish bag.'

'Come on then let's go back you must be hungry.'

'Starving,' grinned Molly, catching sight of Taz in the distance, as she waved he turned tail and ran off.

'Who're you waving to?'

'No one just flapping my arms.'

'Sometimes I wonder about you, my girl,' Mum smiled.

Chapter 44

Because he'd had a good day at the local TV station and the new tie Mum had given him for his first appearance as the weather man, was much admired; Dad didn't mind too much about Molly's scrappy notes from the shore.

'It was raining so hard Dad, I had to shelter under a cover in the dark, so I couldn't see what I was doing,' she said. 'But I've got lots of information stored in my head to write up.' Later her store of information made her go off to her room and draw lots of pictures of Taz in her sketchpad.

The following day as Molly made her way back to the shore, she bumped into Katie coming the other way.

'Hi,' she said shyly.

Katie asked, 'What are you up to?'

Molly told her about the project and was surprised when the older girl said, 'Good luck to you, it's really nice down there today, not many people about.' Sometimes you may see a seal or a dog.'

'Dog?' questioned Molly.

'Er yes, it's a great place for people to walk their dogs,' Katie seemed flustered. 'See you Molly, we're going home today, but we'll be back by next Monday for the party.'

'See you,' said Molly and carried on walking. The first thing she did when she got to the shore was to look around for Taz, but there was no sign of him. She was pleased that Katie didn't seem to think she was nerdy. I wonder how many other kids here or anywhere have to do holiday projects for their parents, she wondered. I bet Katie doesn't have to.

PART 4 MOLLY

Molly got on with her work she found a stick to mark where the tide line was. She drew a picture of the clouds. Today they were big, white and fluffy and moving quite fast up high. The flag fluttered but didn't stand out straight, because it wasn't that windy down nearer the ground. It was blowing in a different direction today as well. Molly was quite enjoying what she was doing and wondered if that's what made her a nerd. She'd brought her watch today and was surprised at how quickly the time went. She'd finished drawing and was just delving in her bag for a drink and a cheesy dip, snack thing, when a woof behind her, told her that Taz had arrived. They were both pleased to see each other and there was a lot of squealing from Molly, tail wagging from Taz and the lovely sound of a rattling snack bag.

The tide came in, quite fast the girl thought as the two friends had to keep moving further and further back towards the bank. Eventually they had to climb up as there wasn't much shore left. They saw a few people coming towards them from the top of the hill, probably to hire a rowing boat. Molly and Taz walked off in the other direction. He obviously wasn't interested in the newcomers and no one called for him. They played chasing sticks and every so often Taz would stop and look towards the sky or the water. Molly followed his gaze and noted the changes of the clouds, the wind direction or the water, in her mind, so she could make some more notes for Dad to look at. Taz noticed what Molly did with her hands, he knew if she was going to pat him, or pull something to eat from her pockets or if she was going to throw a stick for him. They were in tune with each other.

Chapter 45

Surprised at herself, Molly had a lovely week. Mum took her places that *she* wanted to see, not stuffy old museums. She joined in the arts and crafts event, which was on the shore, with a man called Peter and a lady called Rosie. Molly had learnt a lot of stuff while she'd been down there with Taz and surprise, surprise the other kids were interested in what she had to say. In fact they all voted her their leader and after they made a 'Pirate Den,' among the rocks with bits of wood and stuff they'd found, they captured Peter and Rosie, tied their hands behind their backs and made them walk the plank. The two grown ups ended up ankle deep in water and mud. It had been great fun.

Dad was pleased with her project notes and pictures and said he might show them on TV as he was trying to get kids more involved with meteorology—a big word meaning—studying the weather. But best of all, Molly was having a fantastic time with Taz. She'd spent so much time with him outdoors each day she got a bit sun burned. One day she chased him into the river and then had to swim further than she was used to, to try and catch him. He swam next to her and made her feel really confident, so each time she swam a bit further, then they had races back to the shore. One time Molly won.

On Saturday evening after eating, Molly went across to the campsite office and asked the lady there if she could paint a picture for the painting competition.

PART 4   MOLLY

'Of course dear,' said the lady whose name was Sylvia, 'bring it here when you've done and don't forget to put your name on the back and initials on the front.'

'Ok, thanks,' said Molly and went back to the caravan to play card games with her parents. Molly won.

Chapter 46

It was Sunday and although Molly's project was finished, she still went to the shore at eleven o' clock. The tide was in now and there were more people than usual down there, hiring boats. Molly walked along the top of the riverbank, hoping to see Taz, but met Katie and her young brother Josh.

'Are you looking forward to the party tomorrow?' asked Katie.

'I s'pose so. I haven't been here before and I don't usually go to parties.' answered Molly.

'It's fun, they have a mini swimming gala and races on the field during the day, everyone joins in, even the adults. Someone famous judges the painting competition and there's a big barbecue and disco for everyone in the evening, I'm looking forward to it.'

'Only 'cos you love Danny,' said Josh.

Katie went red in the face and Molly smiled.

'I'm going in the running races,' Josh continued and Sam, my brother's going to swim, what are you going to do?'

'Don't know yet,' said Molly, wishing she were good at something. The three said 'see you later' to each other and Molly walked on, thinking about what special thing she could do tomorrow.

Eventually she came across Taz, lying on the top of the bank, looking out over the water. She sat next to him and reached into her pocket for a treat.

'I'm surprised you're not fatter my boy,' she said running her hands over his smooth head and sides. 'I wish I could take you back with me, but you're such a good boy your owner would be very unhappy without you.' Taz lifted his head and licked her hand. 'We're going home the day after tomorrow, I hope we come back again one day,' said Molly 'I just wish I could do something really special, before we go, then Dad won't mind that I only got effort prize at school. Taz just looked at her and licked her chin. 'Got to go now Taz, we're going to visit someone called Jackie and her rescued animals after lunch,' Taz's ears pricked up. 'But I'll see you in the morning,' giving him a last stroke, Molly got up and left.

Making her way back later, Katie saw Josh was already back and playing ball with some other children. She carried on walking, head down as usual when someone shouted, 'I'll get it,' she looked up to see Josh running backwards, his hand stretched in front to catch the ball. 'Look out,' yelled Molly as he got closer and closer to the step, which separated the playing field from the pool. Josh was so keen to catch the ball he didn't hear. He tumbled down the step right next to the post holding the lifebelt, which he bashed into. He dropped to the hard ground and Molly heard a thump as his head hit the floor. As if this wasn't enough of a problem, he rolled into the water and stayed there, face down. This all happened so fast that Molly couldn't have stopped him falling. She ran to the lifebelt and tried to get it off the pegs it was hanging on. One of the other children came and helped her lift it off and without any thought for herself she jumped into the water hanging on to it. Another older boy jumped in and Molly slid the lifebelt towards him, 'Hold this, I'm going to turn Josh over,' she said grabbing the small boy by one shoulder and clearing his face from the water. The water here was too deep to stand up, but by kicking her legs, like she'd been taught and practised with Taz, she managed to hold Josh up with one arm and grabbed the lifebelt with the other.

By now more help had arrived and Josh's dad jumped in, grabbed his son from Molly and took him to the edge where willing hands helped to lift him out. Molly and the big boy swam over bringing the lifebelt and also climbed out.

'Stand back, stand back, I'm a first aider,' said a voice, it was Sylvia, from the office. She knelt by Josh, gently shook his shoulders and said, 'Josh are you alright?'

Josh's Dad stroked the boy's pale face and muttered, 'Come on son, come on.'

As they all watched, Josh's eyelids flickered open, he looked up, saw his dad over him and said in a very weak voice, 'Dad, you're all wet.'

Chapter 47

Once she'd seen Josh open his eyes, Molly ran back to her caravan, to get dry clothes on. She hoped he was going to be ok, he seemed to have hit his head very hard. Mum looked up as her daughter came in,

'What happened to that nice swimsuit of yours?' she laughed.

After Molly had told her what had happened Mum dashed off to find out how the young boy was.

It was some time later that Molly's Mum told her that Josh was fine. He'd been checked over at the nearest hospital and apart from a lump on his head, he had no other injuries.

'I'm so proud of you love, everyone said you were really brave,' her mother gave her a huge hug. 'I'm going to ring your Dad.'

'It's ok Mum, don't disturb him at work, it's his last day today,' said the girl and went back to drawing pictures.

It was late afternoon when Josh and his family stopped by and brought Molly a great big box of chocolates and a DVD token as a thank you present.

'Does your head hurt, you didn't half bash it?' said Molly.

'I'm ok,' replied Josh proudly turning around to show the bandage on the back of his head.

'He'll have to have all the rest of his hair shaved off now,' laughed his mother.

'Oh no,' said Josh, 'I never thought of that.'

PART 4   MOLLY

When Molly went to hand her painting in at the office, Sylvia and Jean were both there and they started clapping when the girl came in. Molly went red but accepted the praise and the thanks and said, 'I wasn't the only one who helped, another boy was there too.'

'That's Max,' said Jean, 'he's a nice lad.' Before they could say any more, Molly's Mum came into the office.

'I just need a quick word with the ladies, Moll,' she said, 'go on back and start packing anything you won't need before we leave tomorrow evening.'

I wonder what she wants to talk to them about, thought Molly but did as she was told.

Chapter 48

The Holiday Park had a big barn, which was used for special events like discos, parties, exhibitions and, sometimes films. There had been lots of people in and out of it all day, putting up decorations, lights and sound equipment, ready for the party the next day. Molly was really surprised when after tea with her mother, Mum said, 'Come over to the barn with me Molly, there's something special happening.'

'Do I have to, it'll be special enough tomorrow?' She answered.

'This is something that won't happen again,' said Mum with a small smile on her face.

Molly's mind went into overdrive; now what?

In the barn a lot of people were standing around chatting, some were sitting on hay bales. Children were having great fun, jumping on and off them or squeezing between them. A massive screen had been set up at one end and Molly thought Great . . . . A film . . . probably one I won't like. Mum pushed her forward, so they would be sitting at the front. Just then the lights were dimmed and the screen came to life, everyone including the children stopped talking and sat still. It was the end of the local news broadcast, and the newsreader was about to introduce the weather forecast.

He said, 'We've had the pleasure of working with Mike Newton, this week, the weather has been exactly what he said it would be. Mike has been asked if he'd like to stay on, in this area but hasn't given us an answer yet. However if he does decide to stay, I would just ask him to find some better ties to wear.'

Everyone in the barn laughed and Molly sat up straighter, her eyes wide behind her glasses, she glanced at Mum, who just squeezed her by the hand and smiled.

'You bought that tie Mum,' Molly hissed.

'I did it as a joke, to see if he'd have the nerve to wear it,' Mum whispered.

Then Dad appeared in front of them, bigger than real life, he was smiling at the newsreader, he fiddled with his tie, then laughed as he faced the cameras. He went over the weather forecast board and said it was going to be a fine day tomorrow. The audience sighed and there were mutterings of things like, 'Oh good,' and 'A brilliant end to the summer season.' Usually when the weather ended, Dad said 'Goodnight' and, the cameras switched back to the newsreader, but not today.

'Before I go,' said Dad, 'I would just like to thank everyone who has made my stay here so enjoyable. I know my family has had a lovely time too, even though I haven't spent much time with them. I wasn't sure if I wanted to stay here or not, but then something happened today, to change my mind.'

Molly looked at Mum.

'I'd like you to watch this,' Dad continued and before everyone's eyes the screen showed Josh, running backwards towards the pool trying to catch a ball. The film continued with the rescue and ended with Molly and Max climbing out of the pool.

'How . . . what?' stammered Molly.

'There's a security camera just opposite where all this happened,' Mum answered. 'It doesn't move around, so we can't see the end of the pool where Josh was lifted out.'

Dad had a big grin on his face and said, 'That brave little girl is my Molly. I am so proud of you sweetheart and I know you've come to love being here in Suffolk, so if you want to, we're staying.'

The audience erupted into loud clapping and cheering and calling, 'Molly, Molly.' Mum had tears running down her cheeks, Molly didn't know where to look. Then she was grabbed by the hand and pulled to her feet in front of everyone. Max held her arm up, his hand in hers.

'Come on Moll, let's give them a bow,' he shouted in her ear, and they did, several times.

PART 5

END OF SEASON PARTY

Chapter 49

Bank Holiday Monday, was a gorgeous day, just like Molly's Dad had said on the weather forecast. The Holiday Park had bright flags flying in the gentle breeze and there were notices about, of what was happening, although most people had already decided where and when they'd be needed.

Jack couldn't wait to get to there again. He and his mum, Lisa had been back to the area a few times, but they'd stayed with Mark, over his surgery. As soon as the car stopped at the park office he was off to go and find Taz, in the woods.

'See you soon guys,' he called over his shoulder to Mum and Mark and then 'come on Nell, come with me.' However Mark's collie dog, Nell stayed where she was, too old to run about now.

Katie got up early and went out for a walk with a pocketful of snacks. She hoped to meet up with Taz, for the last time this season. Her family wouldn't be coming back again until May next year.

Liam was also up early; his gran was already downstairs getting breakfast ready.

'Can I go and look for some blackberries, down by the pond, to have with my cereal?' he asked her.

'It's only half past six are you sure you want to go now, I can't go with you?'

'That's ok Gran, I won't be long,' he said and ran out before anything else stopped him. She watched him go wondering what he was going to put them in, if he found any.

Molly lay in her bed going over and over the evening before, in her mind. She felt really happy and was determined to join in everything she could today. When she was dressed, she crept out of her room and outside into the cool morning, she wanted to find Taz and tell him what had happened. She made her way towards the shore.

Chapter 50

The fun began at midday and everyone taking part had gathered outside the barn to await the opening speech. Mr. Gray, the farmer who owned the park, as usual thanked everyone for coming this year. He said it had been a good season and hoped to see them all again in the future. Finally, to stop the fidgeting children, he held his arms up and shouted, 'Let the games begin.' Everyone who'd been before joined in the shout and lots of laughter and cheering could be heard.

After each race, adults and children gave their names to Sylvia, so they could get their prizes at the end of the day. There were running races, obstacle races, sack races, wheelbarrow races and many more. After the field events, people made their way to the swimming pool and more fun and games took place there. It was a fabulous day.

About four o' clock people made their way to the big barn where a barbecue had been set up outside. The wonderful smell of sizzling sausages and bacon made a lot of mouths water.

Sylvia and Jean were keeping a close watch on everything, they wanted to keep people happy and content, so they'd come back again. Mr. Gray had been wandering about, chatting to as many of his guests as he could, when his wife came over to him holding a phone. Sylvia watched him as he took the call, it was very short and when he'd finished it he looked worried.

'What's up?' said Sylvia

'Our artist, hasn't turned up to judge the kids' pictures, he's still in France. I knew we shouldn't have asked for a celebrity.'

'Let's ask Mike Newton he's well known on TV,' Sylvia suggested.

'No you can't Molly's entered the competition, remember' said Jean. The three stood looking around, wondering what to do.

'You'll have to do it,' Sylvia said to the farmer.

'I can't I did it last year and I don't want to risk picking the same names again, I can't remember who won last year.'

'Hold on a minute, I have an idea,' said Jean and hurried off into the crowd around the food table.

Chapter 51

'Ladies and gentlemen, children, dogs and whatever else is here, please make your way into the barn for the prize giving,' farmer Gray's voice boomed out over loudspeakers.

People made their way inside and there were lots of ooohs and aaahs over the decorations. The children's paintings had been fixed to huge boards, suspended from the beams, and lit up with specially positioned lights. There was a small stage area in front of the paintings, where the farmer stood with his microphone.

Families sat around the long wooden tables, while children jumped up and down trying to see their paintings.

Everyone who had taken part in the field and swimming races won a medal and there were family prizes as well for things like Best Kept Caravan. Hands were getting sore from all the clapping.

'Ok everyone, settle down,' said the farmer, 'when I look at all those little faces out there, I know just how important the painting competition . . .' he paused as a loud cheer went up, 'is, to our youngsters, especially as first prize is a free family week here next year.' Another great cheer. 'Second prize, a free long weekend,' he continued, 'and third prize, all this,' he pointed towards a box full of everything a young artist would love to have. Paper, paints, pencils and an easel.

'Unfortunately, our celebrity artist couldn't get here on time to judge the competition,' some of the crowd booed, 'but we are lucky to have someone even better. Our very own, Maddie Gordon.'

An old lady got up, carrying a large cardboard box and walked towards the stage. She had short silver hair and a very brown face with a big smile on it, making her eyes and cheeks go all crinkly. She was wearing a faded T-shirt, with Save the Animals, written on it, old jeans, that had been cut off to the knees and dusty looking sandals on her feet. Not many people knew who she was but they all clapped and cheered anyway. She took the microphone from Mr. Gray.

'Hello everybody,' she began, 'I'm very honoured to have been chosen to judge your wonderful paintings. I only got back from Africa yesterday, where I've been for a year, helping to set up a new animal sanctuary for unwanted pets. Anyway I know you're all eager to know who has won, so let's get on with it. All the paintings were beautiful and it's been a very difficult decision, but here goes.'

The three winners and their families were overjoyed when they received their prizes and even the disappointed ones still managed to smile and say, 'well done.' Maddie Gordon talked about all the paintings and called each child up, one by one to give them each something from her cardboard box and then she said, 'Nearly finished, but now I'd like to see . . . for want of a better word, the 'Alphabet Bunch.' No one moved, they all stared at her, until she looked at a piece of paper she was holding and continued, 'I've got the initials here, there's JK, a KL, an LM and an MN.'

'That's you Jack,' said Mark.

'Go on sis,' said Sam.

'Hurry up Liam,' said his gran.

'Get up there Molly,' said her mother.

As the four puzzled children made their way up to the stage, the music for the disco began and most of the crowd got up and moved around, children showing off their medals and painting prizes.

Chapter 52

Molly stared at Katie and frowned, 'what's going on?' Katie shrugged. Liam thought he'd done something wrong and kept his head down and Jack stared at the four pictures that Maddie was holding in her hand, she gave the children a big smile, 'Well you four,' she said, 'how long have you been friends?'

'We're not,' said Katie, she was the biggest so thought she ought to speak first. 'Actually, Molly and I were caravan neighbours for a while, but we don't really know each other.'

'Why do you think we're friends?' asked Jack

'By your paintings,' said Maddie and spread them out.

One was a picture of a boy sitting by a pond with his arm round a dog; it was called Me and Taz.

'That's mine said Liam, I'm LM.'

'There's mine,' said Molly pointing to a picture of a dog swimming and pulling a boat with a little girl in it. It was called Taz Rescue.

Jack's picture was called 'Taz and Tam,' it was a picture of a grey and white collie dog, curled around a tiny kitten.

'I did that,' said Jack proudly.

'This must be yours,' Maddie said smiling at Katie, 'Taz Loves Food, what's this big blob, next to a beautiful dog.'

Katie went red, 'that's me,' she said, 'but I'm a bit smaller blob now.'

All four children were absolutely amazed at what they were looking at and they all started talking at once, until

Maddie held up a hand and said, 'Shhh, come and sit down and you can all tell me about Taz.'

They all listened to each other tell their Taz stories sometimes interrupting to say something about him. Maddie understood that, because of Taz; Jack would have a new Dad, when Mum married Mark.

Molly had lost a lot of weight as she played with him and fed him all her rubbish food, so she was much happier and had made lots of new friends.

Liam didn't need a puffer anymore and could play normal rough games and sports with his friends and Molly had made her parents proud of her, which had made her a much happier and confident girl.

'I think that's wonderful, what fabulous stories,' said Maddie and gave them each a little dog pin, to wear on their hats or jumpers. The pins had Save Me written on them. Maddie said they were made for the Animal Sanctuary in Africa.

'It was built to save cats, dogs, rabbits and the sort of animals that we keep as pets. Where I'm working the local people aren't as caring about them as we are. It's been really nice to meet you children, do come and visit me if you like, I'm here for two more weeks.'

'Would you like to keep my picture?' asked Liam, 'I can easily draw another one.'

The other three all said the same thing and Maddie was really happy to be given them. 'Thank you so much, I'll take them back to Africa with me, and pin them on the shelter walls,' she said, 'now go and have fun'

The children turned back towards their families, 'The Alphabet Bunch,' said Liam thoughtfully, 'that sounds cool.'

'Maybe we could have adventures, like in books,' added Molly.

'We won't see each other very often,' said Katie, wondering if her brother Josh could join in.

'Well I'm coming to live near here,' said Molly.

'Me too,' added Jack.

'Gran and Grandad live here, Gran works here,' Liam joined in. 'We come every weekend from May to August, maybe we will all have adventures,' said Molly. 'Let's go and find Taz, together, tell him the good news.'

Chapter 53

As the four children wandered away, Maddie sat on a hay bale looking at the paintings they'd given her. She held them up one by one, a small smile on her face. She felt someone come and sit beside her and a deep voice said, 'I recognise you. Didn't you used to come and visit me at the surgery?'

Maddie looked up, 'Hello,' she said, 'Mark the vet right?' They shook hands.

'Is it really only a year since you went off to Africa? Time goes by so quickly.'

They chatted for a while, Mark was very interested in Maddie's animal sanctuary and she was happy to hear that Mark was going to be getting married. He told her about how he'd met Jack and his Mum Lisa.

'Jack,' she said, 'this Jack?' she held up the picture the boy had drawn. Mark looked at it, 'Yes,' he said, 'Taz and Tam?' He never mentioned Taz to me he found Tam the kitten. Taz, hmm, I know that name too.' He looked at Maddie, 'Isn't Taz your dog, a Blue Merle, two strange eyes, one brown, one blue, did you leave him here?'

Maddie looked away, her eyes misting with tears, 'Yes,' she replied softly, 'I had to leave him here, under his favourite tree in my garden, he died, just over a year ago.'

And that's another story.

EPILOGUE

September

The distant clock was chiming six o' clock, in the afternoon. Suppertime he thought and licked his lips, but he stayed where he was, under his tree, watching the world go by again.

Most of the cars and caravans had gone earlier in the day and he'd heard lots of shouting and chattering coming from the Holiday Park, but now it was quiet and peaceful. The days were getting shorter and soon it would be autumn. Already leaves were starting to change colour and fall from the trees. Not his tree though, it was a sturdy oak, they were always the last to lose their leaves, it would shelter him for a few more weeks yet.

He looked towards the pond and saw one of the ducks chasing another, he would like to have chased it, but he was too comfortable to move.

Across the track someone was calling, 'Ben, Ben, dinner time.'

He looked but didn't see Ben but he did see the lady who lived next door to Ben's family. She walked down the track towards her driveway and just before she went into her garden, she turned and waved.

'Bye bye, see you tomorrow.'

He just looked at her then looked back up the track, to see a large man closing the big farm gate, he lifted his hand and waved at the lady.

The sun was dropping fast behind the trees and it was getting cooler, time to go. He stood up, stretched and started to run back towards his house. As he did so a stray sunbeam, shot across the grass in front of him, he ran happily into it, where it's bright light caught on to something shiny round his neck, a little metal disc, with a single word—TAZ.

----------The End----------

The Author

Pam Tunbridge

Pam's two greatest loves are children and dogs and after a variety of careers she is now a swimming teacher and dog minder. Her first novel Strange Eyes manages to combine her two favourite things in one fantastic adventure. Not only a loving mother, she is also Gran to 2 year old James and is looking forward to a second grandson in the near future. Pam lives with her husband and dogs in a rural area of Suffolk in England. A perfect setting for this novel and the next two to make up the Taz Trilogy.